Lost in Love

EMILY BANTING

Sapphfic
Publishing
www.sapphficpublishing.co.uk

Lost in Love
Copyright © 2021 Emily Banting
Published by Sapphfic Publishing
ISBN: 978-1-915157-01-0
First edition: October 2021

CREDITS:
Editor: Hatch Editorial

1 3 4 5 6 7 8 9 10

ABOUT THE AUTHOR

As an author of LGBTQ+ romance featuring sapphic main characters, I'm passionate about increasing the representation of sapphic women over forty in literature and on-screen.

I write about women in their prime, experiencing everything life throws at them — missed opportunities: regret: lost loves: family problems: aching joints: and menopause.

With a passion for, and a degree in Archaeology and Heritage Management, I never miss an opportunity to sneak historic buildings into my books. The Nunswick Abbey Series features a Georgian country house, a quaint historic village setting and of course, oodles of ruined abbey.

When I'm not hiding behind my MacBook pretending to write whilst secretly consuming tea and biscuits, I bow to the unreasonable demands of my cat overlord and walk my starving velcro Labrador.

Connect with me
www.emilybanting.co.uk

FIND ME HERE

I love to hear from my readers. If you would like to get in touch you can find me here…

www.emilybanting.co.uk

Or follow me here…

 facebook.com/emilybantingauthor
 instagram.com/emilybanting
 twitter.com/emily_banting
 bookbub.com/authors/emily-banting
 goodreads.com/emily_banting
 amazon.com/author/emilybanting

ACKNOWLEDGMENTS

Thank you to all my BETA and ARC readers around the world for taking time out of your day for me. You truly are an awesome bunch!

To those at home that have just about tolerated my absence whilst I've followed my dream. Especially my faithful Labrador who snored by my side the entire time it took me to write this book and took me out for walks when I needed to clear my head.

· Special thanks to Amanda Radley, who not only inspired me to move one hand from screenwriting to novels with her endless collection of epic books, but recommended the best editor a girl can have, Jess.

Jess, your guidance and advice over the last few months has been invaluable, I don't know where I'd be without you. Thanks for crying in all the right places!

Lastly, thank you to my readers who have taken a chance on a debut novelist – I hope it's a worthwhile read.

Rosey,

This one is for you.

You were there at the beginning; may there be no end.

x

CHAPTER 1

*A*nna sprinted through the abbey gate and onto the main road through the village of Nunswick. She had planned out her lunch break meticulously between her two tours that morning.

A glance at her watch told her she had fifty-eight minutes left. Bang on time.

Passing the grand abbey house that lay beside the entrance to Nunswick Abbey, she joined the high street, stepping into the road to avoid a meandering, elderly pedestrian.

Her dad's doctor's appointment was in thirteen minutes. She'd given him strict instructions that morning to be ready for her arrival. He wasn't exactly known for his reliability, so she'd factored in a contingency to be safe.

An unwelcome pain kicked her in the abdomen. A stitch. Despite her best efforts to ignore it, she knew she'd have to take a breather, potentially throwing out her whole schedule. She made a mental note to knock twenty percent off her contingency time.

Slowing to a stop, she regained her breath, blaming the years spent behind a desk in the city for her pathetic level of fitness. Eyeing her garden gate down the road, it mocked her weakness. Pulling herself up straight, she forced herself towards it.

Another check of her watch told her that her dad would need to be ready to go. She pushed the gate open and almost crashed into the front door of the cottage. As she scrambled with her key in the lock, the door opened. Her father greeted her, still in his slippers and cardigan.

"Dad, what did I tell you? I needed you to be ready," Anna said between panting breaths.

"Sorry, love, I must have lost track of time," he mumbled, looking around for his shoes.

"Two minutes, Dad," she barked as she made her way into the small sitting room.

"I was watching *Escape to the Country*. Lovely couple. Didn't buy any of them, though."

Anna placed her hands on his shoulder and made eye contact with him. "That's great, Dad. I'm glad you enjoyed it, but…" She tapped at her watch.

"Oh, sorry, love. I know, you're on your lunch break. Have you had anything to eat? I could make you a sandwich," he said, shuffling towards the kitchen.

"I won't have time and I told you not to touch anything sharp in the kitchen, remember?"

"Oh yes, of course." He held up his shaking hands and moved them around in circles.

"Stop with the silliness, Dad. We need to go now." She breathed heavily, trying to push away the knot she could feel twisting in her stomach. Planning the schedule had kept her mind off the fact that they'd be getting news on her dad's health today. Now that was slipping, she could feel the protective wall she'd built around her crumbling.

"Have you been to the toilet recently?" Anna continued, trying to refocus on the task at hand.

"Oh, yes, I think so," he replied, with the look of someone who was clearly trying to recall the last time they went, remembering a time they did and then trying to work out if that was a memory from today or another day.

Anna guided him to his chair. As she put his shoes on, she reminded herself that she still needed to buy him some Velcro ones that he could put on himself.

During the seven weeks since she'd moved home, she'd realised that, with his increasingly shaky hands, laces were a difficulty for him. He'd initially put up a fight against her helping him but gave in when he tripped over a lace that had come undone.

As she knelt in front of her dad and finished tying his lace, she blinked away warm tears that were stinging her eyes. It always took her back to when she would sit on the bottom step of the stairs as a little girl and watch with fascination as her mum or dad tied her shoes.

She tied them far more efficiently than she had the first time; that had been a strange experience. Not just the physical tying of the laces effectively in reverse to what she was used to but the reversed roles; she was now the parent.

With shoes on, he was ready to take the slow walk over to the doctor's surgery. That element of the job could not be rushed, and she had to walk at his speed. With every short step, though, she fought the urge to lift his small frame and carry him over the road.

They arrived at the surgery with one minute to spare. Anna almost gave herself a celebratory slap on the back but reminded herself that, unless she was back at work on the hour, there was no praise to be had. With timing in doctor's surgeries a law unto itself, everything was still left to play for.

Anna left her father to find a seat whilst she queued at reception. It was a stark contrast to her previous surgery in the city where you acknowledged your arrival on a touch screen. She used the moment to try and calm her nerves, taking deep breaths in and muted breaths out for fear of upsetting the person in front of her.

It had been on a visit four months ago that she realised her dad's health wasn't what it had been. He had markedly slowed down, beyond what ageing would do to a healthy person. His speech, thoughts, and movements had changed, and a shaking in his hand had confirmed her suspicions that, neurologically, all was not well. She had chastised herself for not visiting more often. Life had taken over as it always seemed to.

Her girlfriend at the time, Jessica, hated the countryside and spent most evenings clubbing. There wasn't a club within fifty miles of Nunswick, and the village only had one pub, which was frequented by the over-fifties. Jessica was a few years younger than herself, and Anna couldn't blame her for holding on to her youth, but she had found herself struggling to keep up with her.

Following the realisation that she would need to be in Nunswick more regularly, if not full time, Anna decided that there was no future for them beyond the city. She packed in her much-loved job as a researcher at the National Archives, broke up with Jessica, and moved back home. She chalked the break-up up to experience and decided if she would date again, she would need someone older and wiser, ideally more on her level.

Reaching the front of the queue, a snooty receptionist informed her that the doctor was running about ten minutes behind. She looked at her watch. *There goes the contingency.* The receptionist looked around her to the next patient in what looked like an attempt to shoo her away.

Anna huffed loudly and scanned the waiting room for her dad.

"Ten-minute wait, Dad," she said, collapsing into the seat beside him. She placed a careful hand over his twitching ones.

"I didn't have to wait last time, but she's such a lovely doctor, you'd wait forever and a day." He grinned. "She's what we would have called glamorous in our day, you young'uns would call her 'hot'."

"Dad!" Anna turned to look at him.

"What? I'm a red-blooded male as much as the next man," he chuckled.

The man sitting beside him grinned, as if in agreement with what he had overheard.

Anna examined the waiting room. *This is what it looks like sitting in God's waiting room.* Four men were sat with their noses in magazines, and all looked over the age of eighty. They would have been in their sixties when she left Nunswick twenty-odd years ago; a time when they would have been retiring and playing golf at the local course followed by a tipple after the eighteenth hole. Now they all sat, waiting for the call from above. She shuddered at the thought of what her own future looked like.

She couldn't imagine willingly picking up a copy of *Good Housekeeping* or *Woman's Own* like half the patients there. They were no doubt fighting to get that week's copy, having read the previous week's when they'd been in for their endless string of appointments.

Having the time to read them was another thing altogether; reading was a luxury not afforded to Anna since she'd moved home. As a researcher, she had spent all day with her head in one book or another, often just skimming for particular words, but she got the gist from what she did read and picked up a lot of knowledge along the way. She couldn't help but smile at those simpler times.

The only reading she had managed recently was *The Tour Guider's Handbook*, given to her by the abbey when she first started. A handbook it was not. It was only named as such because someone had scribbled it at the top of the front page in marker pen. It comprised a few photocopied sheets from a book published in the 1930s about the history of the abbey.

During her interview at the abbey, the trustees had explained that Abbey House, the neighbouring property, once included the ruins of the abbey and its land. The developers who purchased it renovated Abbey House and divided it from the abbey, selling them as two separate properties. The trustees had been after the abbey itself for years, unfortunately the price was always too high as it had always included Abbey House.

After having read the few pages from which she had been expected to create a tour, she promised herself she would present the abbey with a more comprehensive version as soon as time would allow her. That was unlikely to happen now. A warmth washed over her as her lungs tightened. Closing her eyes, she inhaled short, controlled breaths, telling herself good things would happen again in time and that she had to focus on what was important now — her dad.

"This is ridiculous," Anna puffed out.

"Don't make a fuss. I'm sure your work will understand if you're a bit late back."

She was grateful for his attempt to reassure her, but he couldn't understand her situation.

"I need to make a good impression; we need this job or you'll be on baked bean rations."

"What will you be on?"

"Thin air, Dad."

He scrunched his face and went back to thumbing through what looked like a classic car magazine but could have been a car magazine that had sat in the surgery since the seventies.

Anna fidgeted in her seat. Noticing there was no queue at the reception desk, she leapt to her feet.

"You said a ten-minute wait. We've been waiting for fifteen minutes now," Anna said, loudly enough for all eyes in the waiting room to turn and stare at her.

"I'm sorry, madam, our doctors spend the time they feel they need to with their patients. I'm sure if your father required more than the allotted time you would want him to have…" The woman trailed off and returned her attention to her computer screen. A grin spread across her face.

Anna frowned at her and was about to chastise her for her insolence when she felt a presence. She turned. A doctor had appeared beside her. Although the same height as Anna, the doctor loomed over her, assisted by a pair of enormous breasts suffocated behind a white silk blouse. Anna went to step back to take her all in but found herself frozen on the spot.

"You must be… Miss Walker? I'm Dr Atkinson, but please call me Katherine. I'm sorry to have kept you and your father waiting," she said, finishing with a smile so wide it created an attractive crease line on either side of her mouth, just below her prominent cheekbones. Her whole manner exuded confidence and glamour.

Anna opened her mouth to speak; nothing came out.

"If you have somewhere more important to be, I can give your father his diagnosis alone?" She gave a little twist to her head and a raise of her eyebrows as if straining to hear an answer she knew wouldn't come.

Again, Anna opened her mouth to speak, but the doctor interrupted whatever may have eventually come out.

"I thought not," she added, looking around the waiting room. "Ah, Mr Walker, if you will?" She gestured towards her office.

Her dad had been correct; Dr Atkinson was something to behold. If Anna hadn't been given a severe ticking-off from her, she might have embarrassed herself with a floppy jaw.

The room was unlike any other doctor's office Anna had been in. It appeared to have been arranged to put you at ease upon entering. Even the cold, metal examination bed was covered in a tasteful throw and cushions, giving it the appearance of a settee. A vase of flowers on the windowsill gave off the scent of a summer meadow and blocked the view of the car park. The only thing that was missing was a collection of candles and background whale music.

Dr Atkinson directed them to two chairs opposite her desk.

"Miss Walker, I see you admiring my décor. Do you approve?"

"Yes," was all the response Anna could manage.

"Who wants to walk into a dreary consulting room, let alone work in one?" the doctor asked rhetorically.

Anna mustered a smile in reply and checked her watch. Half past; time was ticking on. She covered her watch and looked up to find Dr Atkinson's eyes boring into her as she picked up some papers from her desk. Anna bit her lip; she felt like a teenager again.

The doctor tucked her chair in and walked around to the side of the desk, perching herself on the corner closest to her patient.

Anna observed that there was the perfect amount of room on the desk corner that she could perch without knocking anything over. No doubt she used this move on patients to try and put them at ease when delivering bad news. Though, in Anna's mind, it was likely the sight of crossed, stockinged legs and a short pencil skirt that did the easing. Her heart rate picked up as she tore her gaze away. She was more nervous for her dad than she had realised.

"Now, Mr Walker, I have your test results, and it's not good news, I'm afraid. Your scans confirm what we suspected; it is Parkinson's disease."

He lowered his head and nodded in response to his sentencing. Anna took his hand and gave it a reassuring squeeze.

"Early to mid-stage three, I would hazard a guess."

Anna's body twitched as anger coursed through her. "Hazard a guess?"

Dr Atkinson glared at her, as if not expecting questions from the audience at this stage of her deliberations.

"Are doctors always in the habit of guessing rather than working from fact? Can't the scan tell you what stage he's at?"

A flat smile spread across the doctor's face as her eyes softened. "Miss Walker."

"Anna. My name is Anna."

"Anna," Dr Atkinson replied calmly. She put her papers down and crossed her legs in Anna's direction. "Parkinson's is a long-term degenerative disorder which presents with a myriad of symptoms which vary between patients at different stages. Some of these symptoms can even be found in other diseases. We carried out the scan, which I understand you were insistent on, only to rule out other diseases. No test can conclusively show that your father has Parkinson's disease. A thorough physical examination of him had already led us to this conclusion. We cannot cure it, so we simply aim to improve the symptoms with medication. As the disease progresses, the medication can become less effective. There are typical patterns of progression in Parkinson's which we define in stages, and we look to categorise a patient within a stage so we can monitor the speed of the deterioration and prepare patients for what may come next."

Any attempt Anna had made to climb out of her box had been met with a forceful hand pushing her back into it. She was quickly concluding that Dr Atkinson might be the most infuriating doctor she had ever met yet the woman's self-confidence gave Anna confidence in her.

The doctor got up and seated herself at her desk. Taking a band from around her wrist, with one swift motion she placed her blonde, shoulder-length, wavy hair up into a loose bun. She opened a glasses case beside her and placed a pair of black-rimmed glasses on her nose.

Anna sucked in her breath at the sight of her.

"I'm going to give you a prescription, Mr Walker. You'll need to come back in for a review in eight weeks," Dr Atkinson said, looking at him over her glasses.

He smiled and nodded obediently.

Her fingers flew across the keyboard of a laptop, and within seconds a printer behind her was waking up.

"Anna, do you live with your father?" the doctor asked, meeting Anna's gaze, which was still fixed on her.

"Yes," Anna answered, quickly looking away.

"If he has any ill effects from the medication or you notice a change in behaviour, let me know straight away. He should, initially, see some improvement. I would refer you to a Parkinson's nurse, however, we find ourselves lacking in that department. I do have extensive experience with the condition myself, so I'm happy to be your primary contact."

"Well, I'd rather you looked after him…" Anna stopped herself, realising she was saying the words aloud.

The corners of Dr Atkinson's lips curled up.

Anna could have kicked herself for letting those words slip from her mouth. It looked like the doctor knew it as she leaned back in her chair and played with a pen.

"You work at the abbey?" she enquired, pointing her pen at the logo on Anna's sweatshirt.

Anna looked down and swept her long, brown hair behind her shoulder to better reveal the logo.

"Yes. I give the tours," Anna replied, unsure where this new direction of the conversation was going.

"I have a friend visiting this weekend. We were planning on visiting."

"Oh, I might see you, then?" Anna replied with a neutral tone. She wasn't sure if the presence of the doctor at her place of work would be a positive thing.

"Yes, you might." Dr Atkinson smiled again and then wheeled over to the printer to retrieve the prescription.

She passed the slip to Anna, who took it as a cue to leave and helped her dad to his feet.

"Goodbye, Mr Walker," Dr Atkinson said as she crossed the room and opened the door for them. "If you have any concerns or questions, do let me know."

"Thanks, doc," Anna's father replied.

Dr Atkinson narrowed her eyes and smiled at Anna. "It was nice to meet you, Miss Walker."

Anna was about to respond when the doctor shouted

the name of her next patient and disappeared back into her office.

As she guided her dad out of the surgery, she checked her watch. Time felt as if it had slowed down in the doctor's office, and her stomach knotted at the sudden panic that she might be late. She had fifteen minutes to get back to work. Plenty of time to get her dad settled and sprint back to work. Slipping her arm around her him, she helped him across the road.

"How do you feel about it all?" Anna asked as they reached the front door.

"It is what it is, love. No use fighting it, eh?"

"Don't worry, I'll look after you. I'm not going anywhere," she said, giving him a little squeeze on the shoulder.

"I know you will, love, and I'm grateful to you."

"I wasn't here for mum, so I'm going to make sure you get the best care there is, I promise."

As she took the short sprint back to the abbey, she realised that the knot in her stomach was still there, and she knew why. Dr Katherine Atkinson was the most infuriating yet attractive woman she had ever met. She had single-handedly made her feel ashamed and embarrassed by her behaviour. What niggled her most was that Dr Atkinson had no idea why it was her instinct to behave like that around doctors, especially those she didn't fully trust yet.

CHAPTER 2

*K*atherine felt the sun warming her legs. It was only early summer, but with little wind and a secluded patio, it was the perfect spot to catch the sun on a lounger.

Little chirps nearby pulled her attention from her book to the bird feeders in one corner of the patio. They had been one of her first purchases for Abbey House when she bought it a few months before.

The old Georgian house had been extensively renovated by the developers and decorated perfectly to her taste. A few colour coordinating throws and cushions were all that had been required to bring it into its own, and she loved any excuse to buy those.

The host of sparrows perched upon the bird table took off in fright; a small mewing behind her indicated the reason.

"Hello, Virginia."

A small, black-and-white cat leapt onto her lap and pushed itself against her book until she stroked it. She had felt a pang of guilt when she first encouraged the birds into her garden but calculated there must be an endless number of other threats for small birds to deal with. One laid-back cat that spent most of its time asleep indoors would unlikely make for much of an added threat.

Bored of reading — but not of her book, Katherine never bored of reading early twentieth-century women's literature — she snapped it shut and took a gulp of water from her glass. It was warm. This weather demanded something more refreshing than water, and she felt the need to stretch her legs. A walk into the village was in order.

Nunswick's high street had made a big impression on her when she first came to look at the house. So many other villages had narrow, claustrophobic high streets with a poor blend of historical and modern styles. This village held an array of architectural styles, the proximity of the abbey to the high street had likely saved the village from the senseless ideas of modern planners.

Her end of the village consisted of proud, Georgian houses until you reached the quaint, fifteenth-century pub in the middle of the high street. Beyond the pub, several small shops nestled in a row of what were once Victorian houses. They were joined by the library and surgery, both crammed into what was the old Victorian schoolhouse next door.

Opposite stood a long row of small, Edwardian terraces, which she had been informed were owned by the council. Although out of keeping with the historic nature of the village, they were a blessing compared to the more modern council houses that were so often shoehorned into other villages.

People were milling about, chatting over garden walls; they nodded in her direction as she passed. She'd received a huge amount of support from the villagers since arriving, and she had become very popular with patients at the surgery. Overwhelmingly so, with many asking to change doctors as the rumours went around as to her polite bedside manner and welcoming smile. Only working part-time meant she had limited space, and a waiting list had been started, though with the ever-ageing population of Nunswick, the wait wasn't long.

She crossed over the road to the row of shops, all beautifully ordered with large windows beside a door, housed within their gable-fronted Victorian shells. The tearoom was the last shop on the right.

Katherine had been warned about the tearoom and its gossipy owner, Gloria, when she first came to the village. It was the perfect place to let slip a bit of news that you couldn't be bothered to tell an entire village individually. One of Katherine's colleagues calculated that news of her pregnancy had worked its way from the tearoom and around the village in under thirty minutes.

Katherine had avoided the place up till now. Not that she was ashamed of her "news"; she just wanted to give the village time to get to know her before it became common knowledge. People were always more judgemental of those they didn't know.

She pushed into the tearoom and was greeted by a short woman with her hair pulled back into such a tight bun that it almost took her eyebrows with it. From the description she'd been given, she knew this was Gloria.

"What can I get you, love?" she asked with a smile.

Katherine was taken aback by the coarseness of her tone; it wasn't particularly fitting for the type of establishment the tearoom presented itself as. Not one to judge, she looked at the chalkboard beside her and responded.

"One of your vitamin smoothies please."

Gloria grinned. "They're new. You'll be my first customer to try one." She scurried away into a small kitchen behind her.

Katherine examined her surroundings whilst she waited. A business card holder sat on the counter; she picked up one of the cards and examined it at arm's length. It read *Gloria's Lay and Leave Buffet*. Katherine smirked and placed it back in the holder.

It was a relatively small tearoom, quaintly decorated in the post-war style, or possibly just not decorated since then; she wasn't sure. The abbey, she noticed from reading a leaflet she had found in the library, had its own more modern-style cafe.

A gramophone sat in one corner of the small room, with a thin layer of dust on top. Katherine decided it was likely an ornament rather than an entertainment system. Beside it was a small table by a window, with two older-looking ladies sitting on either side, affording them a direct view on to the high street and of the door.

"Don't you mind those two. They're my regulars, the twins," Gloria said, appearing back at the counter with a clear smoothie cup restraining a green liquid.

Katherine did a double take back at the twins, only to be met by the same face and enquiring expression facing her. She did a quick one-eighty back to Gloria.

"You're the new doctor, aren't you?" Gloria continued.

"Yes, how did you guess?" Katherine enquired, knowing full well the news would have spread as to her appearance.

Gloria's head twitched. "Oh, er, lucky guess, I suppose."

Katherine smiled at her and passed her some pound coins. She picked up the smoothie and, encouraged by Gloria's gesturing head, took a sip. It was surprisingly good.

"You know, that's not bad," Katherine said taking another sip. To her, anything was a welcome change from tea, especially in this heat.

Gloria beamed and placed her hands on her hips. "You see, recommended by the doctor herself," she shouted over to the staring twins.

They shrugged and returned their attention to the window.

"You not got a husband joining you? Seems a big house just for one."

Katherine knew immediately she had been correct in avoiding the tearoom up to now, yet she felt she had enough support from the village that she could be truthful. "No, I don't have a *wife* joining me sadly. I'm not married," Katherine replied.

There was a clatter from behind her. She and Gloria both looked over to the elderly twins who would have clearly heard; one was leaning over to pick up a teaspoon from the floor. The other dropped a sugar lump into her tea and focussed on stirring it in.

"Well, you're most welcome here anyway," Gloria added.

Katherine frowned. She wasn't sure how to take the statement but felt sure there must be good intent behind it, so she smiled and thanked her as she left. As she passed the twins, she made sure to give them a smile. In return they eyed her with suspicion.

Luckily, Katherine didn't mind who knew her preferences; if anything it might work to reduce her waiting list of new patients. As far as she was concerned, people could think what they liked about her. They usually would anyway, and she did like accuracy, so it was better that they make informed judgements rather than ill-informed ones.

As soon as she reached the pavement, her phone rang inside her handbag. She placed it on one of the outside tables with her smoothie and delved into it, extracting her mobile. The name "Rebecca" flashed onto the screen.

"Hey, where are you?" Katherine asked, answering it quickly.

"I'm outside your house. Where are you?" came the sharp response.

"Oh, sorry, I popped over the road for a smoothie."

"Smoothie? This doesn't look like the type of village where one can get a smoothie. Am I in the right place?"

Katherine laughed. "Yes, I can see you. Look at the row of shops and you'll see me." Katherine waved, much to the surprise of passing pedestrians.

"I see you. I'll come over; I need a drink after that journey." Rebecca hung up.

Katherine watched as her tall, red-headed best friend navigated her way across the road through her enormous sunglasses.

"Darling," Rebecca shouted as she approached Katherine, arms wide open.

They hugged and air-kissed.

Rebecca lifted her sunglasses onto her head and looked around. "Well, well, what have you got yourself into here? It's beautiful, I'll give you that."

"I did grow up in the country," Katherine reminded her.

Rebecca pulled the corners of her mouth down. "I know. I also know I've lost you completely to it now. There's no persuading you back to the inner city, is there?"

"Afraid not."

"Oh well, you're probably better off here anyway, and I do need a country break occasionally. This looks just the place."

"You know you're welcome any time. Let's walk up an appetite, and then I'll take you for a pub lunch."

Gloria appeared from inside the tearoom to clear a table. Katherine got the feeling that something was always left outside so she could clear it if she needed a better look at something on the high street.

Katherine shoved the smoothie at Rebecca, who took a sip.

She pulled away and examined the green liquid. "That's good."

Gloria grinned.

"Another smoothie if we may?" Katherine requested.

"Certainly."

Katherine and Rebecca followed Gloria inside. Rebecca gawped at the decor as Katherine had.

"What's up with those two?" Rebecca questioned, nodding in the direction of the twins.

"Don't worry about them. They just think we're lovers."

"Are you breaking hearts already?"

Katherine choked down laughter and was glad to see Gloria appear with the smoothie. She popped a note on the counter and passed the smoothie to Rebecca. "Keep the change," she called to Gloria.

Rebecca grinned and took Katherine's hand, leading her out of the tearoom. They burst into giggles outside much to the annoyance of the two faces glaring at them from the window.

"Right. Let's walk and earn our lunch," Katherine said.

Rebecca hooked her arm through Katherine's. "Lead on."

Katherine took Rebecca on the circular walk that started beside her house, then looped around the back of the abbey site and along the river to the other end of the village. They ambled back along the high street to the pub.

"I don't know about you, but I'm exhausted." Rebecca collapsed onto a chair at one of the outside tables overlooking the road.

"It was only two miles. I do it most days, so it has little effect on me. Have a glass of wine to revive you."

Rebecca beamed at the suggestion.

Katherine checked her watch. "Our tour is booked for

two o'clock, so we'd better order." She levelled a look at her best friend. "And you ought to only have one glass of wine."

"Do I have to come?" Rebecca moaned. "Can't I just sit here in the sun and drink?"

"No, you can't! I've been waiting for you to come so I could visit. No one wants to turn up for a tour on their own. I know I'm sad and lonely. I don't need everyone else knowing it."

"You have Virginia," Rebecca teased.

Katherine scowled at her. "Don't bring my cat into this."

"What on earth?" Rebecca said, suddenly surprised. "Is she training for the Nunswick Marathon?"

Katherine turned to look in the direction Rebecca was staring. A figure sprinted past them on the other side of the road and headed into one of the small, Edwardian council houses.

"I think that may be Miss Walker on her lunch break."

"She's cute."

"Is she?" Katherine lifted her eyebrows.

"Like you hadn't noticed. Look at the long, brown hair. Just your type."

Katherine frowned at her. "I think my type is a little more than long, brown hair, thank you."

"Chiselled face, brown eyes? Has she got those too?"

Katherine booted her under the table. "You can see for yourself later. She's our tour guide."

"Uh-oh." Rebecca put her hand to her mouth. "She works at Nunswick Abbey — a history buff too? No wonder you're so desperate to visit."

Luckily for Katherine, a waitress appeared beside them and took their order.

Katherine hadn't — well, she didn't think she had thought about Anna in that way. In the short time she had spent with her during her father's appointment, she had found the woman impertinent.

The waitress disappeared, and Rebecca gave Katherine a look that told her the conversation was far from over.

"I was too busy reprimanding her for her behaviour when I met her to even look at her," Katherine added reluctantly.

"Reprimanding?" Rebecca's eyes widened. "You do know there is a very fine line between your serious schoolmarm persona and you being overtly flirtatious."

Katherine's face dropped. "You don't think…"

"No, but she might," Rebecca answered, nodding towards Anna's house.

"Oh." Katherine clenched her teeth.

Rebecca stretched back in her chair and took in the sun.

"Well, this lifestyle certainly seems to suit you better — pub lunches, abbey tours, walks in the countryside, green goop. Helena would be proud of you."

Katherine dropped her sunglasses down her nose and glared at Rebecca. "Please don't."

"Sorry." Rebecca pinched her lips and zipped them with her fingers.

Katherine had seen parts of Nunswick Abbey from her bedroom window, so she was vaguely familiar with the layout of the grounds. She led Rebecca, who'd had not one, but two glasses of wine, through the visitor centre to the tour pick-up point, as instructed by the young woman at the desk.

Katherine felt strangely nervous; she had been worrying all through lunch that she may have appeared flirtatious to Anna during the appointment when she certainly hadn't meant to - it would have been far from appropriate.

Bang on time, Anna appeared from the visitor centre, introduced herself to the small group, and gave a brief yet informative history of the abbey. She led them off into the grounds, and her group obediently followed.

Rebecca leaned over to Katherine and whispered in her ear. "That's a chiselled face if ever I saw one. And what fine brown eyes."

It earned her an elbow in the side.

Katherine was impressed by their tour guide. She was not only knowledgeable but engaging and humorous, traits Katherine had not seen on their first meeting.

Anna appeared to be avoiding eye contact with her, yet she must have noticed Katherine's presence in her group. Perhaps she had given her the wrong impression and now Anna was embarrassed. Maybe Katherine should rein in her schoolmarm act, she thought. She could see now how it could look flirtatious to men, but surely Anna wouldn't have noticed a woman flirting with her. Not, Katherine quickly confirmed to herself, that she had been.

Katherine felt herself completely drawn into Anna's tour. She spoke so animatedly and passionately about the architecture of the abbey, the people who lived there, and its ultimate downfall during the Reformation. Watching Anna so closely, Katherine realised the tour guide was wiping her forehead regularly. It was warm, sure, but there was a cool breeze. Katherine couldn't help it when her doctor senses began tingling. She moved closer to Anna as they walked on, and when they stopped to admire the north wall of the abbey, Katherine made sure to place herself at the front of the crowd.

Anna was about to restart her talk but began to sway instead, her eyes locked onto Katherine's with desperation. Her arms shot out and her head dropped. Her knees buckled just as Katherine darted towards her and wrapped her arms around her tightly. She felt Anna's body go limp and slowly lowered her down to the ground.

The crowd broke into a round of applause and moved forward to get a closer look.

"Get rid of everyone," Katherine hissed at Rebecca.

Rebecca turned to the group. "Right, show's over, everyone. Please make your way back to the visitor centre to join the next tour or proceed to the next point on your map for a self-guided tour."

The crowd immediately dispersed.

Katherine looked up at Rebecca, impressed.

"What?" Rebecca looked down at herself. "Barrister." She then looked where the crowd had been. "Courtroom."

Katherine returned her attention to Anna. She took a jumper from around her waist and placed it under Anna's head.

"Is she going to be all right?" Rebecca asked, more concerned now that it was just the three of them.

"It's nothing a good meal and a rest won't fix, I'm sure. Have you got any food in your bag?"

Rebecca rummaged and pulled out a chocolate bar.

"Here, I picked this up at the service station this morning."

"Thanks," Katherine said, taking it.

Anna started to come around.

"What happened?" Anna asked, blinking at the sun that was directly in her eyes. "Oh, Dr Atkinson."

"It's Katherine, remember?" she said, helping Anna sit up. "You fainted. Are you diabetic?"

Anna shook her head and tried to get up. "Sorry, how embarrassing,"

"Not at all, and please sit for a minute. Have you eaten today?"

"No, I haven't had time yet."

"Here, eat this and then we'll try getting you up." Katherine passed her the chocolate bar.

"Thanks," Anna replied, stripping the chocolate of its wrapper. The bar disappeared in seconds and the colour returned to her face.

"It's likely your blood sugar dropped. I'd like you to make an appointment with your doctor to make sure."

A member of staff made their way over to them at a trot.

"Hi, I'm Carrie, Anna's supervisor," she said. "I can take it from here; I'm a first aider."

"Katherine's a doctor," Anna informed Carrie.

"Oh, right, good job you were here then," Carrie said, looking relieved and taking a step back.

"Definitely, she caught her," Rebecca piped up.

Anna looked up at Katherine. "Thanks."

"I would say, 'Any time,' but please, no repeat performances. I couldn't follow you around all day; I would never keep up."

A smile danced on Anna's lips.

Annoyingly, Katherine knew that Rebecca was right. Anna was her type.

She turned to Carrie. "Please make sure she books an appointment with her doctor as soon as possible and that she attends."

"I will," Carrie assured her, helping Anna up from the ground.

"And make sure she eats something," Katherine added firmly.

Carrie nodded as she walked Anna back to the visitor centre.

Rebecca put her arm around Katherine.

"Come on, let's get back and open a bottle of wine. I think you deserve it."

Katherine nodded her agreement as she looked over at Anna. She knew she'd need to keep her eyes fixed on her; it would be an easy task. The hard task would be keeping them off her.

Rebecca looked at the fence marking the boundary between the abbey and Katherine's house. "Shame you haven't got a gate. A shortcut always comes in handy, especially when a damsel needs rescuing."

Katherine chuckled. "Hopefully she will have learned a lesson from this, but I fear it's unlikely."

CHAPTER 3

*A*nna tapped the glass of the fish tank from her seat beside it, causing the fish to scuttle to the nearest hiding place. She never understood why doctor's surgeries always had a fish tank. Usually, it was one that looked like the water was never changed and often had a dead fish floating around the top, hardly a good advert for a surgery if they couldn't even keep the fish alive. She'd felt sorry for them as a child. She'd sit next to the tank if she could and watch them swim around and around, trapped. Now she realised she was the fish.

Her fainting episode had given her a chance to stop and assess; it had been a frightening experience. She knew she was overdoing it; she didn't have a choice. There was nothing she could do, and thinking about it just made her situation worse. She felt her lungs tightening as she sat, waiting for her name to be called, and took some shallow breaths.

The worst part of it all was Katherine being there to

witness her collapse, not to mention her posh friend. Anna felt so embarrassed and was relieved to see Carrie so she could escape.

Katherine was a complete contrast to her and obviously wealthy. Carrie told her that she'd caused quite a flutter at the visitor centre after buying a lifetime pass. The new doctor had been the talk of the town when she moved into Abbey House a month ago, only seven weeks after Anna had moved home herself, something she was glad of, as the locals had someone new to talk about, and boy, had they done that. Katherine was self-confident and popular around the village. No doubt she had a string of friends that she would have over for dinner in her enormous kitchen. She was the sort of woman everyone wanted to be, more so as she was so annoyingly beautiful.

All the abbey staff had seen the sales catalogue once the neighbouring house had gone on the market. They had listened to the renovations going on for six months and were overjoyed when it was finally finished. The interiors were sublime; it was everyone's dream house, and with a price tag of one million, it would remain everyone's dream house.

Although Katherine had been kind to her when she'd fainted, Anna had put that down to professionalism; she had simply been doing her job. She would continue to think of Katherine as the snooty doctor who had put her in her place without knowing any of her past experiences. Admittedly she found Katherine attractive. You would have to be blind and insane to not want to spend the night with her given the opportunity. Anna chastised herself, knowing it was wrong to demean the woman to a sex object.

Anna checked her watch, though only through force of habit. She was in no rush to get back to work. Carrie had insisted that she take the time off work for her appointment. Hopefully it wouldn't take long, and she could check in on her dad on the way home.

A door opened; not the one she expected. Katherine walked into the waiting room, and Anna gulped. So much for avoiding her.

"Ah, Anna. Dr Lomax got called to an emergency, so I'm covering his surgery this afternoon. Is that okay?"

Anna stood up before her brain had even had a chance to process this news, and she soon found herself sitting opposite Katherine in her office. She felt as if she had no control over herself when Katherine's commanding presence was around. It was beyond frustrating.

Katherine leaned forward. "Before we get started — "

"I'm sorry, my behaviour… before," Anna interrupted her. She knew that Katherine was going to raise the issue, and she was determined to get in there first to try and lead the conversation. That way she might have some control over it. "I've, we've — I mean, my dad and I." Anna cursed the doctor; she was making her tongue-tied. She tried again. "We've had bad experiences with doctors before. We're a little cautious, to say the least."

"Understandably so. You only want what's best for your father," Katherine replied, visibly shocked by her apology.

"Yes, that," Anna agreed, annoyed that Katherine could state her thoughts more clearly than she could.

"Right, let's see if we can work out what's wrong with you, shall we?" Katherine smiled and stood. "Come over to the couch and let's have that jumper off."

Anna removed her green abbey jumper and sat on the couch in front of Katherine as instructed.

Katherine took the stethoscope from around her neck and warmed it with the palm of her hand.

"May I?"

Anna nodded her consent, and Katherine tucked her stethoscope inside Anna's polo shirt. She could feel the warmth of her hands radiating through her skin and her calm, soothing breath on her face. It hadn't gone unnoticed that Katherine's breasts were directly in her eye line.

"How did you know to catch me?" Anna asked, suddenly feeling the need for a distraction.

"I noticed you had started wiping your brow a little while before. The temperature was warm but not enough to cause heatstroke or for the average person, moving sedately as you were, to work up a sweat."

"You were paying attention," Anna said, looking up at her.

"You were very captivating," Katherine responded. "I moved closer to you to get a better look at you, by which time I could see you were about to faint. I just happened to get there in time."

Anna had never been told her tours were captivating before. She'd had compliments, lots of them, this one was the best so far.

"Well, thank you. You probably saved me from splitting my head open."

"You're very welcome. I'm glad I was there to catch

you," Katherine replied as she moved the stethoscope around.

Anna inhaled whiffs of her fresh, light, floral perfume as she moved; she smelt divine.

Katherine hooked the stethoscope back around her neck and collected a blood pressure monitor from her desk.

"Any possibility you are pregnant?"

Anna laughed. "No possibility." She inserted her arm into the sleeve presented by Katherine.

The room fell silent as the machine did its work.

She knew Katherine must be thinking she didn't have time for sex in her schedule, but as Anna had known she preferred women since puberty, pregnancy was never likely to be in the cards. A shame, as she'd always liked kids, though, at thirty-eight, she knew her baby days were numbered.

A long beep and a hiss of air indicated the machine had finished.

Katherine removed it from her arm. "Well, that's higher than I'd like."

"I don't like doctors' surgeries."

"I got that impression, however, it's unlikely to be the cause." Katherine felt for her pulse on her wrist. "That's faster than it should be too. Was that the first time you've fainted?"

Anna nodded. "I have felt hot and dizzy before. My heart races a lot, even when I'm sat down."

Katherine sighed. "Pop your jumper back on." She returned to her desk. "It's quite clear your body is stressed out, Anna. The symptoms you are experiencing are its way of telling you to slow down." Katherine tapped on her laptop. "Run me through an average daily routine."

"I get up about six, tidy the house, get the laundry on. I wake Dad about half seven, help him dress, get him his breakfast, and then often help him with it. Put him in front of the television. Tidy up again so he doesn't trip on anything. I leave for work at eight fifty and grab a coffee at the tearoom. Work until lunch when I go back to check on Dad. I stop at the shop first if I need to get anything, then prepare his lunch, again helping him with it if he needs it. Tidy up again and get any laundry out. Run him over to the library if I can. Then I head back to work until five. Go back home and prepare dinner, help him with it as dinner is often the messiest. Evenings are a mix of getting him in the bath, folding washing, planning meals, and then getting him to bed about nine. I have two days off a week, and they are much the same without going to work."

Anna looked up at Katherine. She was staring at her in disbelief. It was a moment before she spoke again.

"You work… what, a sixteen-hour day with no breaks, and you don't see a problem with that?"

"Of course I see a problem with it," Anna replied, raising her voice. "What I don't see is a solution. I can't reduce my hours as we need the money to keep a roof over our heads and food on the table."

"Well, what about getting help for your father?"

"Care costs, lots!" Anna replied indignantly. "I've spoken to the council about getting help, but as he doesn't require nursing care, they won't send anyone out. It seems you must be sitting in a pile of your own piss three times a day to gain their interest. All they did was put in a couple of handrails. To them, he is well cared for, by me, and I can't just stop caring to make them start."

The room fell into silence, except for the faint sound of Anna catching her breath. She wondered if she had overstepped the mark with her crudeness. She told herself she didn't care what the doctor thought of her; deep down she couldn't fool herself.

"Do you not have family or friends?"

"Our family are dead, and I don't have time for friends," Anna responded dejectedly.

Katherine chewed at her lips. "It's my turn now to apologise for my previous behaviour, suggesting you might have a more important place to be rather than beside your father. It was unprofessional. I can see you have a lot to deal with."

Anna was taken aback by the apology. Perhaps the doctor did have a heart after all.

"But you need to slow down. Take time for yourself, eat properly, relax, laugh."

"Are you serious?" Anna could feel her blood boiling. "How do you suggest I do that? Where does that fit into the schedule? Others are juggling and struggling, they manage. I just need to work harder at being better at it."

Anna felt a tightness across her chest similar to how she had felt before she fainted. A wave of panic washed over her; she felt hot and rolled up her sleeves. She wanted to get out of the stuffy room, away from the enchanting doctor and her annoying suggestions on how she should live her life.

But Katherine was leaning a concerned face closer to her. "Are you okay, Anna? You've gone pale."

"I'm fine, I just need some fresh air. Can I go?"

"You are not a prisoner here, Anna. You are free to leave when you please, but do think about what I said. You are no use to your father in this state," Katherine said calmly, passing her a prescription from the printer. "I'm prescribing you propranolol. It's a beta blocker for your heart. Take one to two a day and at the same time each day if you can. It will reduce the physical symptoms whilst you work on trying to reduce the stress."

Anna glared at her.

Katherine's expression softened. "As much as you can anyway, and avoid stimulants like coffee."

Anna scrambled out of her chair and headed for the door.

"Please book a follow-up appointment in a week to recheck your blood pressure."

"Why? Nothing will have changed," Anna said, closing the door behind her.

To Anna's surprise, there was a queue at the tearoom. She waited outside in the fresh air until it cleared. She knew the appointment would be a waste of time, but she'd at least managed to check in on her dad, who was sat in front of the television as usual.

"Anna, my darling," Gloria shouted to her when she finally stepped inside. "Usual?"

"You bet," Anna replied. Bollocks to Katherine's

advice. A coffee would at least keep her awake for her last tour of the day.

Gloria fired up the coffee machine and proceeded to make a double espresso.

"What are you doing out at this time? A bit late for lunch, isn't it?" Gloria asked, placing the small paper cup in front of her and squeezing a lid on. "You have had lunch?"

Anna shook her head and placed some coins on the counter.

"I had a doctor's appointment." Anna touched her pocket with the small packet of pills in it. They would have to wait until later; she needed coffee now. A quick Google search whilst she waited for her prescription told her to have one tablet before bed. She never had coffee at bedtime anyway, so she would take one then and see if it had any effect. If it didn't, then she may have to consider taking them in the morning and cutting back on the caffeine.

"I hope you're looking after yourself. How's your dad?" Gloria asked, taking the last sausage roll from the display counter, and placing it in a brown paper bag.

"He's okay, thanks. They've put him on medication now."

"Here, have my last sausage roll. Your mum wouldn't have wanted me to let you go hungry."

"Thanks," Anna said, sweeping it up. She was starving.

Gloria's assistant handed a green vitamin shake to the customer standing next to Anna.

Anna frowned at it. "Gloria, why are you serving snot to customers?"

Gloria laughed. "That's a vitamin shake and very popular with our new doctor."

Anna rolled her eyes; it sounded about right.

"It's so nice to have a female doctor at last, and such a good one I hear. She's one of your lot, did you know?"

Anna stared blankly at her.

"You know" — Gloria nodded — "prefers the lady folk."

Anna nearly choked on a sip of espresso. It couldn't be true, surely, yet Gloria was rarely wrong. Anna tried to act casual even though her heart was pounding.

"How do you know that?" Anna asked, holding her breath that Gloria's answer would hold some actual weight.

"She told me herself," Gloria said proudly.

Anna breathed out; that was the answer she was looking for. It was probably the only bit of gossip she'd ever had straight from the horse's mouth. So the doctor was a lesbian. Who would have thought it? There would be a lot of disappointed men in Nunswick.

She tried to look disinterested, but she could feel her lips starting to betray her. She took a sip of her espresso to hide them.

"Well, must get back to work, I have a tour soon. Thanks for the food, Gloria."

"Any time, darling. Don't want you wasting away."

Anna tried to process the information she'd acquired as she walked back to the abbey. She still couldn't believe it. Not that it affected her either way; the doctor must be at least ten years older than she was, and would no doubt prefer women her own age that had their shit together as she did. No one wanted baggage, and Anna could fill a jumbo jet with hers.

She tried to push all thoughts of Dr Atkinson from her mind as she arrived at the abbey but was unable to stop herself from having a peek towards her beautiful house as she passed.

CHAPTER 4

*K*atherine raked at the gravel on her drive, teasing the weeds away from their hold below. Although her gardeners would carry out the task if she asked, she found it very therapeutic. A few years ago, when things had been rough, Rebecca had advised her to work a three-day week to help reduce her stress levels, but Katherine hadn't realised how bored she'd get with four days off a week, much less how being bored would increase her stress levels.

It was important for her to keep busy, whether it was reading a book, weeding, or just taking a walk, so long as it was calming.

Working on the drive afforded her a view of the high street and the entrance to the abbey, though this did make her feel like a busybody who moves into a village and immediately resorts to curtain twitching. She absolved herself with the thought that she was doing good work with the weeds, and if she could see Anna once a day, she would know she was all right.

Anna's situation had been distracting Katherine all week. She'd been keeping an eye on the appointment list to check if she had booked a follow-up appointment. A week later nothing had appeared for any of the doctors. Katherine hadn't expected Anna to want to see her again — they seemed to clash no matter how she tried to contain the conversation — she had hoped Anna would see one of her colleagues.

Their last meeting had not gone as planned. She had hoped to clear the air, apply a little pressure to help Anna take stock of the situation, but after Anna showed signs of a mild panic attack, things had escalated and Katherine hadn't had a chance to rein them in.

Katherine could understand Anna's frustration; she'd told her she needed to slow down then failed to help her find a way to do so. Anna was short-tempered for sure, no doubt due to whatever was also causing her panic attacks.

She'd been stunned into silence after Anna explained her daily routine, and had even felt the need to take a moment before her next patient. Just hearing Anna's schedule had made her feel overwhelmed.

She had wanted to hug Anna and tell her everything would be okay, but she wasn't sure it would be. Katherine had personal experience with this sort of situation, and if Anna didn't resolve it herself, Katherine knew all too well that something else might. It had crossed her mind to share her past with Anna — surely it would make her rethink things — yet Katherine didn't feel ready to talk about that night, let alone with someone who really was just a stranger.

The sound of footsteps running on gravel drew her

attention to the abbey drive. Anna was on time. She watched the woman as she sprinted down the path. At least she was getting plenty of exercise, especially with the ground she covered on the tour.

The problem was Anna didn't feel like a stranger to Katherine. It had been a long time since she'd found anyone she'd like to be friends with, which hadn't been helped by the year that she completely withdrew from society, but she felt Anna could be one.

Rebecca would be overjoyed if Katherine had a second friend; she regularly raised the subject with her and encouraged her to open herself to others again. If she was going to open herself back up to people, Anna would be a worthwhile candidate.

She resolved to take a new approach. If Anna wouldn't come to the surgery, she would go to her. She knew her last tour finished at four o'clock, she'd read the abbey leaflet about ten times already, so she'd take a stroll around the grounds then. That would give her enough time to finish up in the garden and shower.

Katherine had just finished dressing when her phone vibrated and flashed Rebecca's name. She grabbed at it and mashed the buttons to get the camera on.

"Hey, just letting you know that I've landed safely at Heathrow, you can stop fretting about my plane ditching into the Atlantic." Rebecca's face moved about on the screen.

"I'm sorry for worrying about you." Katherine replied,

with more than a hint of sarcasm.

Rebecca tilted her head. The delay on the screen made her look robotic. "Well, I suppose it's nice to have someone who worries about you."

"You're all I have left to worry about."

"Not made any friends yet then… not even your damsel?"

Katherine frowned at the suggestion. "No."

"Why are you so dressed up? You don't work weekends. You going somewhere nice?" Rebecca's face came close to the phone as if it would give her a better view.

Katherine adjusted her phone so Rebecca could only see her face.

"A girl can dress up at a weekend, can't she?" Katherine replied defensively.

"She certainly can, but not without telling me why."

Katherine tried to keep her voice as casual as possible. "I was just going for a stroll."

"Making full use of the lifetime abbey pass then?"

Katherine rolled her eyes.

"I knew it." Rebecca laughed.

"Right, I'm hanging up on you now."

"Don't forget to put your hair up and your glasses on. She won't be able to — "

Katherine hit the end call button before Rebecca could finish. The screen froze on Rebecca's nostrils before turning black.

She stood and looked at herself in her full-length mirror. Maybe she did look like she was going to work, but she didn't want to appear too casual. Just somewhere between the two would do.

She slipped out of her skirt and blouse, opting instead for a pair of blue jeans, a striped top, and a dark blue jumper to place around her shoulders. She admired herself in the mirror again. Much better.

She opened the top drawer of her dressing table and took out her band. She caught a look at herself in the mirror and questioned her motives. Did she really need the hairband?

She threw it back in the drawer.

Her intentions weren't to seduce Anna. What had she been thinking? Probably reacting to Rebecca's enthusiastic joshing. Katherine settled on the intention of making a good impression on someone she was trying to help, and that she felt perfectly dressed for.

Katherine entered the tearoom just before four. She thought the least she could do was take Anna a drink. She scanned the room and was pleased to see the twins weren't there.

She looked at the menu as Gloria approached the counter.

"Afternoon, Gloria. Can you tell me what Anna usually orders?"

Gloria laughed. "Double espresso!" She folded her arms and narrowed her eyes at Katherine. "She's not been in so often as late. Has that got anything to do with you?"

Katherine grinned. Perhaps Anna had been taking note of her medical suggestions. "Patient confidentiality. Let's make that a mint tea instead."

Gloria laughed again. "You're brave. She won't thank you, you know."

"Perhaps not, but one must try."

Gloria eyed her. "What can I get you?"

"I'll have the same, please."

Gloria was probably right; Katherine wouldn't get any thanks, but she certainly wasn't going to indulge Anna's bad habits. If making big changes in her life was impossible, Katherine could at least encourage her to make small ones. The first challenge, it seemed, was stopping her reliance on double espresso.

Gloria soon presented her with two takeaway cups. "Good luck to you, but I won't hold my breath."

Katherine turned to leave, but then a question came to mind. "Do you know Anna?" she asked. "Personally, I mean."

"I used to babysit her when she was little. Knew her mum ever so well."

"Did something happen to her mother?"

"Oh, I'm not one to gossip. You'll have to ask her, or better still your colleagues."

Katherine smiled and made a swift exit. She hoped Gloria wouldn't say anything to Anna. She'd gleaned from Anna that the family had a problem trusting doctors, at least she now had an inkling that it concerned her mother. If Anna's mother was deceased, the records at the surgery would be closed, and she had no reason to request the password. She'd have to trust that Anna would tell her one day, though she couldn't focus on that just yet; getting through to her today was going to be a challenge itself.

She took the short walk to the abbey and was greeted

cordially by every member of staff that saw her. News must have got around about her purchasing a lifetime pass to the abbey. It was hardly a large cost, but she felt it was as worthy a cause as any. Just from her bedroom window, she could see the work that went into its upkeep. As it was an independent charity, she knew they needed all the help they could get.

She spotted Carrie at the desk and approached her.

"Dr Atkinson, how lovely to see you. You have a pass, so you don't need to come to the desk. You are free to come and go as you please."

"Thank you, but I was hoping to catch Anna. She has just finished a tour, correct?"

"Yes, she'll be up at the far end."

"Is it okay if I catch up with her? Just a quick check-in, you know."

"Oh yes, please do." Carrie nodded. "To be honest, I've been a bit worried about her since she fainted."

"Don't worry. I'll look after her."

Katherine exited the visitor centre and set off to the top end of the abbey. She regretted getting hot drinks now; although it was a cool day, the heat from the cups was burning into her hands.

She found Anna sitting in the ruin of the chapel. She was in a small, low window frame, her back to the side and her legs stretched out along the sill, gazing out of what remained of the window. She looked peaceful yet burdened.

"Hello," Katherine called out softly.

Anna jumped.

Katherine approached her. "Sorry, I didn't mean to

make you jump. I'm glad to see you resting, but perhaps you shouldn't be sitting down on the job."

"I was just taking five minutes. Doctor's orders if I remember correctly," Anna replied sullenly.

"You'll find no argument from me."

"I don't remember making an appointment."

"You didn't, and that's exactly why I'm here. Don't fret; I cleared it with Carrie."

"I heard you bought a lifetime pass; you're practically royalty now."

Anna swung her legs around and moved up. Katherine took the hint and sat beside her.

"Look, I'm sorry if we got off on the wrong foot when we first met. I get told I can be a little intimidating. I get a lot of questions; especially with the internet, everyone thinks they're a doctor."

"I get it, and yes, we did," Anna said softly.

Anna seemed different to normal, not that Katherine knew what her normal was, she seemed dejected and spiritless compared to their previous meetings. It saddened her to see Anna like this; her spirit was one of her most attractive qualities.

"Here, it's not coffee. I couldn't bring myself to buy one." Katherine handed her a cup. "You know it's basically an addictive poison."

Anna took the cup from Katherine. "Thanks. I thought it was supposed to prevent heart disease."

"It can also cause heart disease; it really depends on your genes."

"I'm sure you didn't come all the way from over there

to talk to me about coffee." Anna gestured towards Abbey House with her head.

"No, I came to see how you're doing and in hopes you wouldn't do a runner on me again. I'm not sure I'd keep up; I have a few years on you."

Anna gave a weak smile. "I'm still alive, less so kicking."

"Have you tried the tablets I prescribed?"

"Yes, they've actually helped. Thanks."

"Good. I hate to bring it up, and please don't shout at me, but I've been thinking about your predicament all week. Have you thought about a care home?" Katherine asked cautiously.

"Am I that shouty?" Anna said, her head dropped.

Katherine regretted her choice of words. She was really concerned now.

"You do know your father's condition won't improve, right? It will gradually worsen until he needs full-time care."

Anna suddenly broke down in tears. It wasn't something Katherine had expected; Anna had seemed such a hard nut that she'd thought the direct approach was best.

"I'm sorry, I didn't mean to upset you," Katherine said.

She wasn't sure what to do, so, listening to her instincts, she placed her arm around Anna and pulled her closer. Anna willingly and surprisingly collapsed against her. Katherine placed her cheek on Anna's head and held her tight as she sobbed. Katherine was close to tears herself; she knew what Anna was going through, and it brought back painful memories.

Anna pulled away and sat up.

"I just… I just can't face it, after Mum."

"What happened with your mother, if you don't mind me asking?" Katherine hoped Anna would share; she was desperate to know what was haunting her so much.

"My mum had been suffering from stomach pains and nausea for a while. The doctor said it was indigestion. Then it got worse, and I came to visit and noticed she'd lost loads of weight. It was so gradual Dad hadn't noticed. If I'd just been here more often, not so bloody busy with my job, I might have realised what it was."

Katherine's hand shot out to Anna's. "Stomach cancer."

Anna nodded. "By the time they worked it out, which they only did after a lot of shouting from me, it was too late. She spent the last few weeks of her life in a care home. It was a hell hole. I'm not doing that to Dad."

"The time will come when you can't cope anymore. You must see that." Katherine braced herself. She knew any questioning of Anna's ability to cope with her caring responsibilities would likely trigger her; it was a common occurrence.

"Of course I see that," Anna said, raising her voice. She stopped and took a deep breath before she carried on more calmly. "I try not to think about it. I'm not a rich doctor who can summon up the best care in the world without a second thought. I don't expect you to understand my predicament, we are very different people from different walks of life, so please don't tell me what I will or won't be able to do."

Katherine knew she'd overstepped the mark, and she

hadn't intended on adding to Anna's distress, ` she was glad that Anna seemed aware at least of what the future looked like.

"I'm sorry, I don't mean to question your abilities. I'm concerned that you shouldn't have to keep trying to cope. It's not a life, and I'm sure it's not a life your father would want you to have."

"I know." Anna tried to wipe her tears with her hand.

"Here, I have tissues."

"Thanks."

Anna wiped her eyes and blew her nose. A mewing sound followed.

They looked at each other.

Anna laughed weakly. "That wasn't me."

"Nor me." Katherine smirked.

Virginia pushed her way between them from behind, having jumped up into the windowsill from outside the chapel.

She walked straight to Anna's lap and sat down.

"Hello again," Anna said, stroking the cat.

"Again?" Katherine asked.

"Yes, sometimes she comes on my tours. Only the afternoon ones, though. I've noticed she's never around in the mornings."

"That's because she's tucked up on my bed and doesn't get up until lunchtime." Katherine narrowed her eyes. "You traitor."

Virginia miaowed back.

"Oh, is she your cat?" Anna asked.

"She is; this is Virginia."

Virginia mewed on hearing her name.

Katherine stroked her, and she purred at her touch. "I'm sorry if she's any bother."

"She's no bother, are you?" Anna said in a silly voice as she stroked Virginia under her chin. "I love cats, but my ex-girlfriend was allergic."

"Oh." Katherine gasped, looking up at her. "Oh, that's a shame," she added quickly. She bit her lip. Anna's declaration had completely taken her by surprise. Her mind raced, but at the back of her head, a voice screamed, *Deal with it later*.

"Anna, I promise you I will do my best for your father."

"A lot of doctors say they will do their best, but when it comes down to it, their best just isn't good enough."

"Well, I hope to reassure you that that's not me. Have you tried getting a small network of locals together to help you? Neighbours? Your father must be loved within the community."

"He is, but people make promises and break them. They have their own lives, their own problems to deal with. I've learnt that we're better off on our own."

"Well, you need to start trusting more. I'm going to give you my mobile number. Give me your phone." Katherine asked, holding her hand out.

Anna took out her phone and handed it to her. "You are bossy."

"I am. Don't cross me."

Anna laughed, tucking her hair behind her ear.

Katherine tapped at the phone and passed it back. "Look, I may be your father's doctor, but I'd really like to be your friend. If you can squeeze me into your hectic schedule."

"I'd like that," Anna replied, trying to withhold a smile but failing miserably.

"Good. Us lesbians need to stick together."

"Oh, are you..." Anna started to question unconvincingly.

Katherine nudged her with her body.

"As if you didn't know," Katherine interrupted her to save her any embarrassment. "I told Gloria over a week ago; everyone in the village knows by now."

Anna smiled. "Maybe avoid the phrase *stick together* next time."

Katherine thought for a moment and then pulled a face. "Drink your tea. It's good for you. No more coffee."

Anna did as she was told. "Not bad, but I can't promise you'll convert me."

"How many coffees do you have a day?"

"It was about eight, I suppose, but since I started taking the tablets, I've reduced it as instructed."

"Good, keep going. That much coffee could be the cause of your high blood pressure. That and stress, but the latter we seem to be able to do less about... for the moment anyway."

"We?" Anna questioned.

"Yes, we're friends now, and friends help each other, right?"

Anna smiled and nodded her agreement.

Katherine stood. "Come on, Virginia. You can walk me home."

Anna lifted Virginia from her lap and passed her to Katherine.

"Remember, call me any time," Katherine called out as she walked away, chuffed that she had finally broken through Anna's outer defences.

CHAPTER 5

*A*nna hesitated at the counter. It was something she'd never done before; she'd always had the same drink since she arrived in the village. Now she was wracked with indecision.

Katherine's voice was in the back of her mind telling her to get a mint tea, her own screaming forth for coffee. She'd had a coffee that morning when she got up, so perhaps it was now time for mint tea. *Coffee! Even if it's decaf, get coffee.* She closed her eyes to calm her conflicting thoughts. Katherine's smiling face appeared, causing a rush of warmth to wash through her.

"Coffee, darling?"

Gloria's voice shocked her back to reality.

"No, mint tea, please," Anna requested quickly. There were audible sighs in the back of her head.

Gloria chuckled and put her hands on her hips. "I'll be damned. Under the doctor's spell already, are we? That was quicker than I'd given her credit for."

Anna smirked. "I don't know what you mean, Gloria."

Gloria continued chuckling to herself as she poured hot water over a teabag.

Anna stepped out onto the high street with a tingle in her stomach, unsure if it was the thoughts of Katherine's smile or the three-month review she had with Carrie in fifteen minutes.

She was pretty sure there weren't any problems with her work; she'd bent over backwards to make a good impression, and everyone seemed to like her. She had given a guided tour to a group of the abbey trustees the previous week, and they all shook her hand and thanked her for a stimulating tour.

It had been a few days since Katherine had visited her at the abbey, and although Anna had been initially surprised, she was glad she had come. Their previous meetings at the surgery had not ended well, and it was good to have cleared the air. Anna had tried to push thoughts of Katherine to the back of her mind when she found out she preferred "the lady folk", as Gloria so aptly put it. She had been entirely unsuccessful in this endeavour; every spare moment was filled with pondering where Katherine was and what she was doing.

When she materialised like a gorgeous apparition through the ruins, backlit by the sun, Anna thought she was imagining things. More so when Katherine declared she had been thinking about her all week — well, about her predicament anyway, which was basically the same thing.

Although she had broken down in front of her after a tiring day, Katherine had been nothing but supportive, and

Anna had realised she may have been wrong about her. Her manner could be a little pushy, but it came from a place of kindness, and she felt her calming voice alone could cure anything. She'd nearly melted when Katherine put her arm around her and pulled her into her. She could have happily remained pressed against her soft and squidgy body, but didn't want to embarrass herself by leaving tears on her top.

Anna waited outside the meeting room in the abbey's visitor centre. It was a small centre but packed a punch with its cafe, which in her mind served terrible coffee, an open-plan ticket office, two administrative offices, a meeting room, and a staffroom. It had won an architectural design award within a month of opening, much to the delight of the trustees who must have invested greatly in its construction.

Carrie popped her head around the door beside Anna. "We're ready for you."

We? She hadn't been expecting anyone other than Carrie for her review. This was a bad sign, she was sure. If they were going to sack you, there was usually someone from human resources in attendance.

Anna followed Carrie into the meeting room. A woman sat at the end of a long table. Anna recognised her as one of the trustees from the tour and let out a sigh of relief at the appearance of a potential fan. A trustee wouldn't get their hands dirty with a firing.

She stood to greet Anna.

"I'm Margaret, one of the trustees," she said, shaking her hand and gesturing to the seat to her left.

Carrie took the seat opposite her and gave Anna a

reassuring smile. "Well, Anna, the trustees have been hearing great things about you."

"Good," Anna replied nervously, unsure what else to add.

"I just wanted a little chat with you," Margaret said. "Carrie will then go through the formalities with you of your review. All right?"

Anna nodded.

"As you know, Nunswick Abbey has been open for six months and has already been a big hit beyond the local area. The trustees have been taking stock over the last week to see what we need to do to improve things, make things more efficient, and increase our offering if you will." Margaret danced a little in her seat as she spoke. "Now, as I'm sure you know, your tours are very popular. Who knew tours could be so engaging, but somehow you managed it."

Anna braced for the "but" she was sure was about to come.

"But we need more of them, and we need more of you, Anna."

Anna felt a strange mix of delight and defeat. She knew her tours were good, but there was no more of her to go around.

"I can't work any more hours," Anna said, keen to confirm her position on the matter.

Margaret lifted both hands up from the table.

"What we have planned won't involve any additional hours, just more responsibility. We'd like for you to become a tour supervisor. If you accept, we'll hit the button on recruiting two more tour guides, whom you will train and supervise."

Anna hadn't expected that. A promotion within three months of a new job, surely that was unheard of.

"There is one further request we have of you — an Abbey guidebook. It would follow the basis of your tour for those that want the information but without the tour itself. I've looked at your CV, and you have all the skills and more, I'm sure."

Anna couldn't believe it; she'd be able to achieve what she wanted and more, all whilst being paid, and possibly more than she was now.

"The current tour is, I understand, approximately twenty minutes?" Margaret turned to Carrie for confirmation.

Carrie nodded her agreement.

"We'd like to push that to forty minutes. We really need to be more of a destination, keep people here longer, make it more of an afternoon out rather than a passing-by. We're looking to expand the food and drink facilities to offer meals rather than just hot drinks and snacks; visitors will come for lunch and leave on a cream tea. We're really excited for our new phase, and we'd really like you on board."

Anna was overwhelmed, giddy from excitement and nervousness. It wasn't an opportunity she could or would turn down; after all, she said no additional hours.

"When do I start?" Anna replied with a nervous smile.

"Right away, if you will?" Margaret stood and packed a few papers into a bag. "I'll leave you with Carrie now, but I look forward to working with you more."

"Likewise. Thanks for believing in me."

"You're well worth it, I've been assured." She nodded at Carrie and smiled.

They shook hands, and Margaret headed to the door.

"Margaret," Anna regretted speaking up as soon as she said her name, but she had no choice but to continue as Margaret had stopped to listen. "The coffee in the cafe is terrible."

"Thank you for your honesty. I'll look into it."

As the door closed behind her, Anna let out a big breath. "I was not expecting that."

Carrie laughed.

"What about you?"

"I'll still be your manager. They've basically just moved everyone up a peg to keep the experienced staff and will add another level at the bottom."

"Dare I ask if a tour supervisor gets paid any more?"

"Yes, and you'll now be a site key holder," Carrie said, pushing some keys towards her.

Anna picked the keys up. "That sounds like a bit of a responsibility."

Carrie laughed again. "You'll be fine, trust yourself. You'll be on an on-call roster. It works out about once a week among us all. So far I've never had a call out."

"The Abbey guidebook, when can I start on that?" Anna asked, her eyes alight with excitement.

"I knew you'd be dying to get your teeth into it. Start whenever you like. Once you've worked out the text, you'll be working with a designer to pull it together. Use this room if you need to when it's free."

Anna nodded.

"Right, let's get the boring paperwork out the way."

Anna was elated; she couldn't wait to tell her dad. Her new friend Katherine would be another challenge altogether; perhaps it would be best to keep it from her until she could prove the responsibility wouldn't be too much for her. It wasn't as if she was likely to see her again until her dad's next appointment.

Anna held her dad's arm steady as they crossed the road to the library. Once a week she would take him over so he could change his books for the following week.

This time she was keen to get there herself. She was dying to get her hands on some of the local history books so she could really get to grips with the history of the abbey. Although she had already delved into the history for her current tour, now they wanted double its time, so she'd need a lot of extra material to fill it out.

She'd already filled her dad in on her promotion. He was, as she'd expected, pleased for her. He hadn't questioned whether it would involve more hours or time away from home. Anna knew she'd never given him a reason to believe she wouldn't be there for him when he needed her.

As they entered the small library, Anna inhaled the air; there was a familiar scent to it.

Katherine's perfume.

"Hello, Anna. Hello, Mr Walker," Katherine said, appearing from behind a shelf laden with books.

"Call me Harry, won't you, doc?"

"Of course. As long as you stop calling me 'doc'."

"Agreed, but I can't promise I'll remember tomorrow. It's like *Groundhog Day* up here," he said, tapping his head.

Anna and Katherine exchanged a glance. For the first time, Anna felt awkward around Katherine. The atmosphere felt different between them since Katherine insisted on handing over her phone number — that, and them both knowing the other liked the ladies. It felt charged. It seemed they were into the first awkward stage of friendship where neither party really knew how to be around the other.

"You have a look around, Dad, whilst I check these back in," Anna said, patting the large bag slung over her shoulder.

Her father nodded. "I'll leave you ladies to it. Anna, you can tell her all about your promotion."

Anna could have strangled him.

"Promotion?" Katherine enquired, eyebrows raised.

"Before you start about me managing — "

"I wouldn't dare," Katherine interrupted with a sly smile.

"It's the same hours."

"More responsibility?"

"Yes, but good responsibility. I'll have two tour guides to help once I've trained them up. They also want me to write an Abbey guidebook."

"I'm pleased for you; honestly, you deserve it. Hopefully it will be a load off you, which is what we're aiming for."

"Thanks," Anna replied, reeling from just talking about her news. It hadn't escaped her that Katherine had used the word *we* again. "Did you know they are planning on expanding the visitor centre? It's very early stages."

"I didn't, no."

"Well, I'm here for local history books," Anna said after a choked silence. "The tour is expanding to forty minutes, and I need material to fill it."

Katherine nodded, and Anna headed over to the history section. She pulled book after book into her arms, pleased that there wasn't a lack of resources. A quick check of her watch applied some unwanted pressure. She looked around for her dad, only to spot him chatting with Katherine.

"Come on, Dad, we need to get going. I've got to get back to work."

"Sorry, I've kept him talking," Katherine said. "It appears we are both fans of spy fiction, and we were just comparing notes. If you need to go, Anna, I can walk him home. I've nothing on this afternoon."

"I can't ask you to do that," Anna replied.

"You didn't ask; I offered." Katherine stared her down with a look clearly meant to remind Anna to rely on others more.

"You can stop for a cup of tea," Harry offered, blissfully unaware of the tension.

"He means you can make him a cup of tea," Anna added.

Harry grinned. "She's most welcome to stop for one too. I'd enjoy the company."

Katherine grinned back and looped her arm around his. "So would I. It's a date."

Anna rolled her eyes. "Don't encourage him!" She

hadn't told her dad that, despite being too old for Katherine, he didn't stand a chance with her because he wasn't her type. "If you're sure it won't put you out? He uses a beaker for his tea. I'm sure he'll show you."

"I've had experience with Parkinson's patients before. Don't worry."

Anna felt a sense of relief at being able to get back to work on time. She gave them both a smile and hurried off to the checkout counter, keen to get her head in the books as soon as possible.

Anna had never been so grateful for the walk home being so short. She'd taken the maximum number of books from the library at lunchtime and had contemplated leaving some in the meeting room at work but decided against it in case she could manage to get an hour to work later that evening.

She knew it was unlikely, but she was excited to get back to where she had left off on medieval Nunswick. She knew she would have to contain her excitement until tomorrow when she could get back to it between tours.

Having been so preoccupied with her new project, she hadn't even thought about dinner. Her nostrils flared at an aroma coming from one of the neighbouring houses. Her stomach rumbled, reminding her she'd skipped lunch again.

She turned the key in the door and opened it, only to be met with the inviting aroma at full strength. She drew in a nervous breath, wondering if her dad had decided to try and make dinner again.

Anna blinked and wondered if she'd walked into the right house. It was tidy and clean. The raucous laughter of her dad came across the living room as he watched the television; it was the right house.

Anna hung up her coat.

"You all right, Dad?" Anna asked, admiring the tidy sitting room.

"Never better," he replied. "Can you smell that? Proper grub."

Anna was about to question what the food she provided him was but was more intrigued by what was going on in the kitchen to bother. She entered the kitchen cautiously, unsure what she was about to find.

What she did find was Katherine, apron strapped on, hair tied back, with glasses perched on her nose. Anna felt her whole body fizz at the sight of her and gulped. It took her a moment to even question her presence, but she eventually gave way under the weight of the books she was holding.

"What's going on?" Anna asked, setting the books on the dining table. "I thought you were just going to see him home after the library. You must have been here all afternoon" — she leaned down to peer through the glass door of the oven — "cooking lasagne."

Katherine removed the apron and placed it on the back of the kitchen door.

"Before you shout and tell me I'm overstepping the mark, which I completely understand I am — "

Anna interrupted. "I'm not shouting. I probably should

be, but someone told to me watch my stress levels and I don't like to cross her."

"Well, he explained how he'd been struggling to read lately as he can't turn the pages as well, and one of the library books he chose I wanted to read, so it made sense for me to read it to him. I hope you don't mind."

Katherine sounded a little flustered, and Anna found she enjoyed watching the doctor squirm for a change.

"And the lasagne? I don't even have the ingredients to make that in the house."

"I nipped to the shop," Katherine replied sheepishly. "Look, I enjoy cooking, but I have no one to cook for. You and your dad are practically doing me a favour. Speaking of favours, you can do me one in return actually."

Anna grinned. "Oh, here we go; now it all comes out."

Katherine laughed. "No, I just wanted to come back and read to Harry, if you don't mind."

"Are you doing this because I was promoted and you don't think I can handle it all?"

"No. I know by now not to question your abilities. I'm doing it as I'm lonely and I'd like some company. Plus, we're book buddies now." She nodded towards Harry.

"She's reading to me," Harry called over to Anna, not taking his eyes off the television.

"I can't let you do all this. You barely know me."

"Well then, we need to change that, starting with dinner at my house. How does Saturday sound? Bring your books if you need to." Katherine tapped the pile on the table.

Anna squelched her initial joy at the offer of dinner

with Katherine and a tour around her palatial pad. Surely Katherine knew she wouldn't want to leave her dad alone.

"Harry can park himself in front of my fifty-inch television," Katherine quickly added as if reading Anna's thoughts and needing to clarify. "I'll even throw in a bottle and a full Abbey House tour. I bet you've been dying to have a nose."

"Perhaps you do know me," Anna replied, twisting her lips playfully.

"I know your type," Katherine teased.

"What do you reckon, Dad?" Anna shouted around the door, relieved that the invitation included him.

"I'll be there even if you're not," he answered, still not taking his eyes from the television.

Katherine was right; she was dying for a nose around the historic house, but she also found herself wanting more of the doctor's company.

"Okay, on one condition: I need to do a bit of market research on my current tour, work out what works, what doesn't."

Katherine cocked her head. "I'll do my best, but my tour guide was a bit flaky. She even fainted in the middle, but apparently, they still promoted her."

"Well once she gets the new tour ready, perhaps she could give you the first tour," Anna replied.

"I'll hold you to that." Katherine nodded at her. "Right, well I'd better be getting home."

"You're not joining us for dinner?" Anna asked, disappointed.

"Nope, I'm going to leave you in peace. Plus, I've made enough for four so you can have leftovers tomorrow.

Lasagne always tastes better the next day anyway, so I apologise in advance for the awful meal tonight."

"Apology accepted, I'm sure it will be totally inedible," Anna joked, walking her to the door. "Seriously, though, thanks for today. I haven't seen him this happy in a long time, and thanks even more so for the food. You honestly don't know what it means not to have to cook for two days."

"Any time. It's nice to have someone to cook for. You'll be able to squeeze in a few extra hours of reading now." Katherine turned towards her patient. "Bye, Harry. It was good reading with you today."

Harry raised a shaky hand in the air.

"I'll see you Saturday," Katherine reminded Anna as she walked up the path.

Anna felt her chest tingle; she attributed it more to the excitement of having time to read later that evening than to the thought of having dinner with the hot doctor at the end of the week.

CHAPTER 6

Katherine hadn't realised how nervous she would be. It was only dinner after all, so why she had changed outfits three times already, she wasn't sure.

Virginia mewed her disapproval at all of them from the bed

"Shush you," Katherine replied on her last outfit change, having finally decided it was the one.

She settled on a floral summer dress, simple but elegant. She didn't want to appear too casual; it wouldn't be good if it didn't look as if she'd made some sort of effort, but then again, what was classed as too much effort? She wondered what Anna would be wearing, whether she was having the same dilemma.

Katherine picked her phone up and tapped out a message to Rebecca.

Damsel, dinner, tonight!

She waited.

1 friend + 1 friend = 2 friends, good luck! Keep me posted x

Rebecca was right; this was just friends getting to know each other better. Although Katherine knew she found Anna attractive, she also knew they could never be more than friends. Any relationship could be considered unethical. It could also have consequences. So, why was she bothering to try and look nice? *To give a good impression*, came the reply.

She tidied away the discarded outfits and cast her eye around the room. All clean.

She regretted offering Anna the full tour, realising that would mean she would have to make sure everything was clean. It wasn't as if the house got untidy as such, but the amount of dust was unbelievable, and it had taken most of the day to lift every trace from all the rooms.

She had contemplated getting a cleaner when she first moved in, but unlike the garden, she thought it was manageable. Why she'd decided to buy such a big house, she'd never know. Perhaps she was still harbouring dreams of filling it with voices. Or perhaps with so many rooms, it was easier to imagine that there were other people in them and she wasn't alone.

Anna stood nervously at the door, her dad hooked on one arm. Her insides were churning.

Harry nudged her. "Go on then, ring the doorbell."

There was no doorbell, only a rather grand knocker. Anna did a double take at it after using it. It was a partially naked woman surrounded by two serpents made from antique brass, subtle enough that only those with an interested eye would notice it.

A breeze blew around Anna's bare legs; it was cool for a summer's day. She had felt a dress would work as somewhere between casual and smart. She'd only thought that morning about what she should wear, though she realised she only had a few summer options anyway, so she decided to dress down a smart dress with sandals. It had been months since she'd been anywhere other than work or around the village; it was nice to get a little dressed up for a change.

Katherine opened the door and Virginia made a quick exit through it.

"Welcome, come in."

Anna felt a lump in her throat at the sight of Katherine and swallowed hard to try and get rid of it.

Harry crossed the threshold and passed Katherine a bunch of flowers he had hidden behind his back. "To say thank you for the best lasagne I've ever had." He winked at her.

"Thank you, but honestly you didn't need to."

Anna followed behind him. She could feel Katherine's eyes bore into her.

"I don't think I've ever seen you out of uniform; it suits you. You should wear your hair up more often," Katherine added.

Anna grinned at her. "So should you."

Katherine smirked and took her coat.

"I love your door knocker by the way."

"Rebecca got me that as a moving-in gift."

"Is that who came to the abbey with you?"

"Yes, that's her."

Katherine led them across the expansive hallway into the sitting room. Anna hung back to take a few deep breaths to calm herself. It didn't work; the breaths were infused with a hint of Katherine's perfume, and she felt her heart pound harder in her chest.

Harry stood open-mouthed at the ridiculously sized television in the corner of one end of the sitting room.

"Has it got all the channels?"

"All the channels you could want and more." Katherine guided him to a comfy-looking leather armchair beside a fireplace. Beside it was a small table and a reading light. Anna assumed that was where Katherine would settle herself in the evenings. The room was so big there were two large sofas sitting opposite each other with a table between them at the other end. That looked more like an area for entertaining.

"Here." Katherine placed a remote in his hand and gave him a quick run-through on its use.

Anna examined every inch of the room whilst Katherine was distracted. She particularly wanted to see if there were any photographs around that might indicate if Katherine had anyone special in her life.

There were no photos, just several landscapes hanging from the large walls.

Anna slipped a sandal off and pushed her foot into the plush carpet, stopping herself before the groan inside became involuntary externalised.

"Come through to the kitchen," Katherine called over to her.

Anna quickly slipped her sandal back on, hoping

Katherine hadn't noticed, and followed her through a pair of French doors into a show-home kitchen. Light grey cabinets ran the full length of the walls until they reached a wall of bifold doors that opened onto the garden.

"Take a seat." Katherine gestured to the marble-topped island in the centre of the room.

The pop of a bottle made Anna jump. Katherine placed two flutes on the work surface and filled them from what Anna presumed was prosecco, but on closer inspection, the bottle appeared to be champagne.

Katherine slid one over to Anna. "Cheers."

Anna lifted her glass to meet Katherine's and then took a sip. Whatever it was, it tasted great.

"I'm glad we went with flowers now instead of a cheap bottle of wine. I thought you would have expensive taste."

"When you don't have anyone to spend money on, you end up spending it on yourself. Then you develop an expensive taste. I'll get dinner started, and then I'll show you around."

Katherine flitted around the kitchen pulling dinner together whilst Anna watched.

"I hope you're not going to too much trouble for us."

"Nonsense, but I did settle on my one-pot lemon chicken to free me up a little."

Scratching at the patio doors caught Anna's attention. "It's Virginia."

"Could you let her in for me, please?"

Anna got up and opened the door. Virginia scurried in, and, noticing Anna, she pushed into her legs before running out of the kitchen.

"Do you not have a cat flap?"

"Well, Virginia had cat-flap privileges revoked in our old house. She's a mouser."

Anna wondered if she meant *ours* as in Katherine and Virginia or as in Katherine and someone else.

She stepped out onto the patio and examined the garden. The lawn was extensive; a long fence ran to the end of the garden marking the boundary with the abbey. Virginia was a lucky cat.

Katherine poked her head around the patio door.

"Right, come on, it's in the oven. I've got something to show you upstairs that I think will make you weak at the knees."

"You have my attention."

Anna followed her back through the sitting room.

"All right, Dad?"

"Never better."

He had a plastic cup with a lid and straw coming out of the top with what appeared to be beer beside him. Katherine had thought of everything.

She led Anna up the ornately carved wooden staircase.

"I'm already weak at the knees from this staircase; I'm not sure I need to see anymore." Anna stroked the handrail as she climbed.

"You'll want to see this," Katherine teased.

Anna followed her into a bedroom at the top of the stairs.

It was the biggest bedroom Anna had ever been in. What she estimated must be a super-king-size bed was against one wall; opposite was a floor-to-ceiling glass frame protecting a wall of wattle and daub.

Anna walked over to it, mouth wide open. "O. M. G. Imagine waking up to that every morning."

"Yes, imagine," Katherine added.

That sounded like an invitation to Anna, but she thought she must be mistaken. She examined the wall, her nose almost pressed to the glass and her hands reaching out to something she knew she couldn't touch.

"The house was pretty much in original condition until the war. The government took it and the abbey over, and the house was ripped apart. The developers said this was the only original internal wall left, so they made a feature of it."

"They certainly did." Anna looked around the room. "Is this your bedroom?" Anna noted there were no photographs up here either. If Rebecca was her girlfriend, then they couldn't be that close.

"Of course. There's an en-suite and dressing room through that door," Katherine replied as she walked over to the window. "The only part the house the developers didn't restore was the coving. I found some images of the original ceiling moulds in the local archive, so I aim to restore them all myself."

Anna pulled herself away from the wall and joined her. The light was fading, but she could make out part of the abbey to one side. The garden was even more amazing from above, and the views over the countryside were breathtaking.

"In this one spot, you are surrounded by so much beauty," Anna said. She sensed Katherine's gaze on her and turned to face her.

"I am," Katherine replied.

They stared at each other just long enough for it to feel awkward.

"I imagine most would be envious of what you have," Anna said, trying to break the silence and turn her attention away from the butterflies in her stomach.

"A big, empty house is nothing to be envious of," Katherine replied wistfully. "A small house with love and laughter is far more enviable."

Anna blinked. She was right of course, but the way she put it was heart-breaking.

The rest of the tour included four further enormous bedrooms and either two or three bathrooms, Anna couldn't keep track. Downstairs there was a music room with a grand piano, which Katherine admitted she could barely play, and a study which Katherine left Anna in whilst she attended to dinner.

Anna examined the books lining its walls, intrigued by what interested Katherine. It was a mix of history, covering everything from the prehistoric period through to the Cold War. Her fiction section was just as widespread, with Shakespeare at one end and Ian Fleming at the other.

After dinner, Harry parked himself back in front of the television with another beer. Virginia had taken a shine to him and was curled up on his lap.

Katherine topped up their champagne as they sat at the kitchen island and Anna quizzed her on the tour.

"Finally, presentation."

"The best bit in my opinion. Your passion and enthusiasm for history shone through; it's your strongest asset. You just have to work out how to clone yourself. You could have spoken about any subject and you would have enraptured people."

"You're saying it's not what I said, it was the way I said it. Wow, I might as well throw all these notes in the bin then if they're of no interest."

Anna made moves to screw up her notes. Katherine placed her hand on hers to prevent her. Their eyes locked the instant their hands touched.

"Don't be too hasty." Katherine laughed. "That's just my opinion."

"Perhaps it's just you that is enraptured?"

Katherine's face dropped. She paused for a moment, then removed her hand and stood up.

"Are you okay?"

"I have a sudden headache." Katherine put her hand to her temple. "Too much champagne perhaps."

Anna looked at her watch politely. "I suppose we should get going anyway." She packed her bag up quickly, not entirely sure what she'd done wrong. Katherine put her hand on hers after all. Had she backed her into a corner with her question and scared her? Whatever it was, the atmosphere had suddenly changed.

Anna shouted, "Dad, we're off now."

"All right." The sound of the last dregs of beer being sucked through a straw came from the sitting room.

Katherine closed the door behind them and ran upstairs to her bedroom. She grabbed the phone beside the bed and tapped at it before holding it to her ear. She paced the room.

"Sorry to ring so late, Becks."

"What's up? You sound a little panicked. Take some deep breaths."

Katherine sucked in air. "I'm not sure I can do this."

"The damsel?" Rebecca questioned.

"Yes, the damsel."

"If you don't want to be lonely, then you know you're going to have to open back up, Kat. That's part of friendship. We discussed this, remember?"

"I know, but I don't think this is friendship."

Her declaration was met with a moment of silence.

"You have feelings for her?"

Katherine closed her eyes and drew in a breath. "Yes. She's amazing, funny, selfless, but I can't. I can't go through it again, Becks. I can't."

Her eyes flooded with tears.

"Okay, look, everything is fine. You don't have to do anything you don't want to do. Take a step back. Do you want me to come down?"

"No, no, it's fine. I just don't seem to be able to control myself around her. My heart got me to this point, and now my head can't deal with what it's supposed to do."

"Your head is supposed to listen to your heart."

"But what if… it happens again?" Katherine's voice trembled.

"You can't live by what-ifs! Have you explained your situation to her?"

"No, she knows nothing; I'm sure she'll lose interest. She has enough problems of her own without mine."

"So you don't want her to lose interest?"

Katherine flopped onto the bed. "No, I really, really like her. I can hardly concentrate when she's around. I have the overwhelming urge to scoop her up in my arms and kiss her every time I see her."

"Then you have to open up to her. If she's worth having, she'll be there for you."

Katherine nodded and wiped her eyes. "Okay."

"I'm here, remember? Any time. Let me know how it goes."

"Thanks, Becks. Night."

"Night."

Katherine hung up. Rebecca was right; she was going to have to tell Anna everything. The problem with baggage was that, although you could keep it zipped up and private most of the time, on occasion you would have to unzip it and fling it open for others to examine.

CHAPTER 7

*A*nna checked her watch. It had barely changed from when she'd checked it moments before. Katherine was still late for her tour.

Although she hadn't seen her for over a week, she knew she'd been in to see her dad as he'd spoken of little else after, but she was always gone before Anna returned home. She had wondered if Katherine was avoiding her. In the end, Anna texted her to say her new tour was ready, and to her surprise, Katherine replied within minutes.

Thoughts of that night at Katherine's house hadn't left her mind. She ran over and over it, wondering what she had done or said that had upset Katherine. She could only think that maybe she had overdone the flirting; she certainly hadn't believed Katherine was experiencing a sudden headache.

One thing Anna had come to realise was that Katherine knew so much about her life, yet she knew nothing beyond the fact she was the local doctor who'd moved into the biggest house in the village. She enjoyed cooking, spy fiction, and had a cat called Virginia. It read like a contestant introduction on a game show.

She'd learnt very little more from spending an evening at her house. She wanted to ask more questions, yet something prevented her, and she trusted her instinct not to push it. Katherine chose not to share, and although intrigued about her past, and how she could afford such a big house as a part-time doctor, Anna knew she would have to wait for Katherine to reveal parts of her life as she felt able to.

Anna checked her watch again, unsure if she was annoyed Katherine was late, worried that something might have prevented her from coming, or if she was just impatient to see her again. She couldn't blame her for keeping a distance, especially if she was trying to deal with her own issues.

The site was a little eerie with no one there; the rest of the staff had already left. Anna felt it would be better to test the tour out when the site was closed but part of her also couldn't pass up the opportunity to have Katherine to herself.

Rather than follow the old tour route that led guests around the site in a loop and straight back to the visitor centre, where they would inevitably leave, Anna had decided to weave them through the site and then leave them at the far end, allowing them to wander back in their own time. After Margaret's comments about the length of time guests were staying, she felt this would help keep people on-site longer. With changes planned for the visitor centre, guests would now have to go back through it and past the gift shop and cafe before leaving. All she needed now was someone to try it out on before unleashing it on the public.

She heard the crunching of the gravel underfoot before she saw her. A flush of warmth spread through her body, a mixture of relief and possibly lust as she came into sight.

"Sorry! Surgery was running a bit late, and then Gloria insisted on me checking one of her moles." Katherine popped down two cups on the picnic bench. "I'm parched."

Anna released a silent breath of relief.

"Decaf, right?" Katherine smirked as she moved one cup towards Anna.

Anna grinned. "Right, thanks. And thanks for coming."

She wasn't sure whether she should mention their previous parting; it seemed it should be up to Katherine to mention if she wanted to. Katherine sipped at her drink; assuming she wasn't eager to unburden herself, Anna decided to begin. "Okay, this run-through is not for timing, just content, so if something doesn't feel right, speak up."

Katherine nodded her understanding.

"And be honest," Anna added.

"That I can do," Katherine replied.

Anna checked her watch; a rough idea of timing wouldn't go amiss.

Before long, the tour was going better than Anna had hoped. Katherine was laughing, taking part when required, and pulling all the right faces. Anna couldn't be more pleased, especially with the amount of work she had put into it.

When they reached the end, Katherine had no negative

comments to make. "It was superb, the right amounts of everything."

"You're sure?"

"Yes, I have no lingering questions. It was clear and concise."

"Okay, one last thing to run by you. How do you feel about dressing up?"

Katherine coughed into her hand. "Dressing up?"

"Yes, like nuns?"

"Oh, I see. It would feel strange having you dressed as a nun giving that tour. You would be expecting it from the first-person point of view, and then that would feel out of place with a seventh-century nun talking about the abbey during the war."

Anna pinched her lips together. "I'm not sure we could do outfit changes mid-tour. One to ponder maybe. You'll notice the tour ends up here now rather than by the entrance."

"Perfect. I can wander back at leisure and take another look at anything that particularly interested me."

"Yes! Shall we?"

They strolled back along the manicured lawn.

"I took your advice today," Anna said after a few minutes of silence.

"Indeed?"

"I cloned myself. Two new recruits raring to go."

"If they can match your enthusiasm, all the better; it's hard to teach."

"That's what I thought. They were the two least experienced, not that you need much experience for a tour guide. They just had something about them."

"Do you ever get bored repeating the same information day in and day out?"

"No. It might be the hundredth time I've done a tour, but it will be the first time a visitor has heard it."

Anna's fingertips danced along a stone wall as they passed the main section of the abbey.

Katherine observed her with a smile. "When did you become so interested in history?"

"Have you been over to Halsey Castle?"

Katherine shook her head. "No, but I've heard of it."

"The three of us used to go up there when I was little. Dad would chase me around, and then we'd have a picnic and feed the leftovers to the ducks. I guess I connected with the place, and soon I was obsessed with history."

"And what is it about historic buildings particularly that gets you so… fired up?"

Anna laughed. "History is a window to another world, a world where I can never go, but the buildings, being pretty much all that remains, allow me to feel closer to history." Anna stopped and patted the stone wall. "Now, spoiler alert, I'm a bit of a control freak."

"Surely not. You don't seem the type at all," Katherine teased her.

Anna narrowed her eyes at Katherine. "So, in a way, history is my nemesis. The past is totally beyond my control. I hate that; it's a place I can never go. But I can learn from it, and that helps me to control the future better, in a way. Take this building, for example; if you could hear all the voices that were absorbed by the stone, what would they tell you?"

"No end of things, I imagine," Katherine replied.

"Exactly, and it's our job to listen. Understanding what came before is such a valuable but underused resource. Learning about the past simply makes me feel part of it, and thus I conqueror my nemesis." Anna hesitated before continuing. "The more you tell me about your past, the more I can... understand you."

Katherine glanced at Anna but didn't respond; she didn't need to. Anna knew she had planted the seed of thought in her that she wanted her to share, and that was enough.

"So, have you always been a tour guide?" Katherine asked.

Anna laughed. "No. I kind of fell into this when I knew Dad needed me here full time. He suggested writing to the abbey to see if they had any jobs. I was hoping for something more in marketing and events, which is what I've mainly worked in, but they only had the tour guide job. As I'd worked as a researcher at the National Archives, it seemed like an interesting challenge. I enjoy it, but I do miss the buzz of events."

Anna thought now would be a good opportunity to push Katherine a little. If she pushed back, at least she would have good reason to take issue with her after all her questioning.

"What do you enjoy other than reading? What keeps you occupied of a weekend?"

Katherine walked on; Anna fell in step beside her.

"I walk a lot. I enjoy audiobooks."

"Lazy reading," Anna replied curtly.

Katherine opened her mouth at the suggestion.

"What else?" Anna asked with a grin before Katherine could argue the point.

"I'm good at taking pity on the overworked."

Anna pushed her lips out and slowly nodded. "Good to know our friendship is being built on pity."

Katherine appeared instantly remorseful at what she had said. "To be honest, it's not. Not on my part anyway. In that way it's built on envy."

"You envy me?"

Whatever lay beneath Katherine's surface must be tragic if she envied Anna's life.

"You have someone to care about."

Anna knew she was right. When life was boiled down to its component parts, that was the backbone of it. She was about to respond, but Katherine got there first and changed the subject.

"How are you doing? Medically, I mean."

"I feel fine. It certainly helps knowing I have someone reliable to fall back on if I need it. Literally, in some cases."

Katherine smiled. "This new tour must have taken a lot of work. You must have written it in, what, a week?"

"Pretty much, but I had a lot prepared from when I created the tour originally. It was more a case of making everything I had cohesive."

They reached the bench by the abbey entrance, and Katherine lifted her bag onto it.

Anna eyed it suspiciously.

"I know this isn't exactly professional, but do you mind if I just check your blood pressure?"

Anna knew it wasn't worth the effort to put up a fight and so she sat, placing her arm on the bench.

Katherine extracted a box from her bag and proceeded to strap the machine onto Anna's arm. "Thanks, if only to put my mind at rest that it hasn't gone up."

The machine whirred away until it finally hissed.

Katherine pulled her lips straight. "Okay."

"Just okay?" Anna raised her eyebrows.

"Yes, just okay. It hasn't gone up at least." Katherine put the machine back in her bag. "I was chatting to your dad, and he asked if I could take him to the library in future. He says he always feels a little rushed, and as it's one of the few times he gets out of the house, he'd like to spend more time there."

Anna shrugged and stared at her feet.

Katherine continued. "I also wondered if I could take him out a bit more. Maybe for a walk down the high street or to the tearoom?"

"He's a grown man. If he wants you to take him, then... that's fine." She knew it was a positive move. There would be less for her to deal with, and he would be happier. A sadness swept through her.

"Anna, I got this." Katherine placed a hand on her shoulder. "He still needs you and will very much continue to."

"I know." Anna nodded. "Thanks for being there for him, for us."

Katherine squeezed her shoulder before letting go. "Right. If you're done with me?"

"Yes, thanks for coming."

"No problem, I enjoyed it."

"I'll see you soon, maybe?" Anna raised her eyebrows hopefully.

"No doubt." Katherine stood still for a moment as if deep in thought, then flashed Anna a smile before walking away.

Anna watched her, feeling deflated they hadn't made any arrangements to spend time together again. Katherine was so difficult to read it was infuriating.

Katherine suddenly stopped and retraced her steps to Anna.

"I need to apologise for my erratic behaviour the other night."

Anna looked at her blankly.

"The headache," Katherine reminded her.

"Oh, the headache." Anna grinned.

"I'm sorry, I got a little… spooked." Katherine retreated backwards along the path.

"So, are you saying you are enraptured?"

Katherine hesitated. "I might be." The corners of her mouth turned up. "But I do have a past."

"I get that. I'm here if and when you're ready to tell me."

Katherine nodded. "Thanks."

She turned again and was away. Anna felt every step of distance that was between them.

CHAPTER 8

*K*atherine extracted herself from the shower and dried herself with a plush towel. Large, fluffy towels were one of her must-haves in life. She detested hotels where their offering was a thin, rough, miniscule towel that she couldn't wrap around her. It was part of the reason she always booked a five-star.

As she entered the bedroom, her phone lit up and vibrated against the bedside table. It was late for Rebecca to be calling. When she examined it, though, "Anna" flashed up on the display instead. She answered it quickly.

"Katherine, it's Anna. I'm sorry to ring so late, but you said any time."

"Of course. Is Harry okay?"

"What? Yes, Dad's fine. He's in bed. There's an emergency up at the abbey, and I'm on call."

Katherine walked to the window and looked out. Her bedroom only afforded a view over the back end of the abbey site, but she couldn't see anything other than darkness.

"I have to go. Could you come over in case Dad wakes up? I don't want him to find himself alone."

"Oh, yes, of course. I'll come straight away."

"Thank you."

Katherine hung up and redressed. It had only been a few hours since they had parted company after Anna's tour, but little else had occupied her mind since.

The front door was ajar when she reached Anna's cottage. She tapped lightly and pushed the door open.

Anna emerged from the kitchen, torch in hand.

"Thank you so much for doing this. I'm sorry to have to ask for help."

"It's fine. Honestly, I was only going to read in bed. Your sofa is as good a replacement as any."

"I doubt that. I have seen your bed, remember?"

Katherine cleared her throat. "Well, you better get going."

"Yes, help yourself to the kitchen. I'm sure you must know where everything is by now."

"Thanks."

Anna made her exit, leaving Katherine in the sitting room. She placed her book on the coffee table and looked around. She didn't like to pry, but on one of her book-reading visits to Harry, she'd noticed a photograph on the windowsill that she wanted to inspect more closely. It was a photograph of Anna and her parents on holiday; Anna must have been about twelve. It was nice to put a face to her mum, but it was one she'd seen already — it was Anna's face looking back at her. It must have been hard for Harry to see his wife's face in his daughter's every day, but perhaps it was soothing seeing her live on in someone else.

Katherine collapsed onto the sofa and picked up her book.

Katherine felt something stroke her face and opened her eyes to see Anna crouched beside her.

"You looked so peaceful. I didn't want to wake you, but I'm not sure you'd ever walk again if you spent the night on that sofa."

Katherine stretched and yawned. "I must have dozed off," she replied, sitting up.

'Thanks again for coming over. You're a lifesaver."

"As I said before, I'm here for you."

"Thanks, it means a lot. I'm going to make a hot chocolate; do you fancy one?" Anna asked as she walked into the kitchen.

"Please." Katherine followed her; she wasn't in a hurry to leave Anna's company even if it was late. "Is everything sorted at the abbey?"

"It was a break-in. They've secured the site, and the investigators will be back in daylight to assess any damage. It looks like some kids got in with their car. I'm surprised you didn't hear anything."

"I did just take the longest shower known to mankind. Why are you even on the roster when you're also a carer? Surely they wouldn't ask a single mother to be on call?"

"Probably not, but then Dad's not a child."

"No, but he is a vulnerable adult and therefore a

dependant. I suppose you're still expected in work first thing."

Anna shrugged. "I can't rock the boat, especially when I've only just got a seat in it."

Katherine felt angry on Anna's behalf. It seemed to her like the trustees were taking advantage.

"If you are getting paid more, wouldn't it be worth looking again at getting some care in?"

Anna chuckled grimly. "No raise would be enough to allow me to pay for care."

"I don't believe you," Katherine remarked, irritation breaking through her voice despite her best efforts. "You said it yourself, you're a control freak. You won't allow yourself to trust anyone else; then if anything goes wrong, you only have yourself to blame."

"That's easier than having to blame others, isn't it?" Anna questioned.

"No, Anna, it isn't! It's hell!" She fought to keep her voice down. "I know you think I could never understand your situation, but I've been where you are. I've had people telling me to slow down. I ignored them, just like you are, and I've dealt with the fallout. I must face myself in the mirror every morning knowing I could have done something and I didn't. It eats you up inside." Tears rolled down Katherine's face. "I'm sorry." She sniffed.

"It's okay." Anna rubbed her arm. "There are tissues out there. Go and sit. I'll bring these chocolates through."

Katherine nodded and went through to the sitting room. She quickly tried to compose herself and wiped her face with some tissues. A stirring sound came from the kitchen. She stuffed the tissues in her pocket. Anna had opened her home to her, her father, and her heart; perhaps it was time to let her in a little. Especially if it would help Anna see reason.

Anna entered and placed two mugs on the table before sitting beside her on the sofa. She shuffled herself around until she sat sideways and faced Katherine.

"What was her name?" Anna asked softly.

Katherine took a deep breath and looked down.

"Helena," she paused, realising it had been some time since she'd said her name aloud to anyone.

She felt the soft touch of Anna's hand on hers; it gave her courage to continue. She took another deep breath, determined to fight back the tears so she could speak properly.

"We'd been together about eight years; she was younger than me, and we were both getting on a bit. I was already working ridiculous hours, trying to provide for her. I wanted her to have the best of everything; she deserved it." Katherine felt herself rambling and paused.

Anna squeezed her hand and rubbed the back of it soothingly with her thumb. "It's okay. Take your time."

"She wanted a baby, we… we wanted a baby. I worked every hour I could get; the stress I put myself under was phenomenal. I refused to listen to anyone when they told me to slow down. IVF is expensive; a baby is expensive."

Katherine could feel her jaw and throat tensing. She inhaled deeply to try and relax them.

She raised her head and looked at Anna. "Well, I had a heart attack."

Anna's grip on her hand suddenly tightened. "Shit."

"Luckily, I was in the right place at the time. I was

working in the urgent treatment centre at the hospital. Helena wasn't so lucky. They called her, and she came straight to the hospital, but she never made it."

Anna covered her mouth with her free hand. Katherine could feel her tensing through the other.

"Her car was struck by a drunk driver a mile from the hospital. She was killed instantly. She had been eight weeks pregnant."

Anna froze.

Katherine grabbed another tissue from the box and looked at Anna's face. Tears were rolling from her eyes too. Katherine passed her the tissue and took another for herself. "You okay?"

Anna blinked and wiped her eyes. "Am I okay? Shit. You've been carrying that around inside you all this time, and you ask if I'm okay. Can I hug you?"

Katherine nodded. She didn't just need a hug; she needed a hug from Anna.

Anna shuffled closer to her and wrapped her arms around her.

"I'm so sorry," Anna mumbled into Katherine's hair. "If I'd have known, I would have kept a distance, flirted less."

They separated but remained close.

"So you admit you were flirting?"

Anna laughed. "I... yes. All while you're mourning your dead girlfriend."

"Wife."

Anna rolled her eyes. "I'm an arsehole."

Katherine laughed. "Don't stress about it. Honestly, don't! You weren't to know. I should have let you in earlier, but you have your own stresses and... it's hard to talk about. You piece yourself back together, or in this case my best friend does, and you worry talking about it will pull a piece out and you'll fall apart again."

"Tell me you're not going to fall apart from telling me."

"I don't plan to, but hopefully now you can understand where my head is at. It's a little bit more cautious than my heart. It may take a bit more convincing to let go of the past."

Anna nodded. "Is this why you're into country living now?"

"Following doctor's orders to rest and reduce your stress levels when you are mourning your dead wife was a struggle. Especially when you are surrounded by the life you had together. I'd also realised when she'd gone that I had nothing — except Rebecca, of course. She picked me up and helped me rebuild a new life here but with strict rules. She's sort of like a sponsor."

"It's great that you have Rebecca, but do you not have any family?"

Katherine shook her head. "My father died when I was little, and my mother died of cancer two months before Helena. We never got the chance to tell her we were having a baby. She desperately wanted to be a grandmother." She twisted her lips. "The irony was my mother left me a wealthy woman; I didn't need to be working so hard, but it helped me forget she was gone. I should have stopped, and I didn't. Now I have to live with that."

She lifted her finger to Anna's jaw, applying a light pressure to close her gaping mouth. Her finger wandered and stroked the side of Anna's face. Anna took her hand and pressed it to her lips.

Katherine felt a flutter in her chest.

Their eyes locked.

"I'm so sorry all that happened to you. I'm here for you too."

Katherine smiled and withdrew her hand slowly. "That's also part of the problem."

Anna frowned. "How do you mean?"

"Since all that happened, I found the best way to protect myself was to make sure I couldn't get hurt again by losing anyone. It's not by accident that I'm lonely; I choose it. But I'm finding as time goes on, I like it less."

Anna nodded. "Now you're opening yourself back up to possibilities and you're…"

"Running scared. I hope you understand."

"Completely." Anna tucked her legs underneath her. "Since we're being honest, I want to discuss what you said about me."

Katherine shut her eyes, embarrassed to think about it. "Sorry."

Anna reached out to her and placed a hand on her knee. "No, don't be. You're right, I am a control freak, but I'm trusting you with Dad. That's a big deal for me."

"I know. I'll give him the best care, as a doctor and a friend, but please take heed from what's happened to me. We all have our breaking point, and we usually don't know where that point is until it's too late."

Anna nodded her agreement.

Katherine gulped the last of her hot chocolate and stood. "I better be going. It's very late."

Anna walked her to the door and held it open.

"Thanks for listening," Katherine said, turning to face her.

"Thanks for sharing, finally."

Katherine felt the urge to hug her good night just as Anna reached out to her. Katherine responded and closed her eyes, inhaling the scent of Anna's hair and enjoying the pressure of her body against her own. They clung on to each other longer than was necessary for a farewell parting. Katherine eventually pulled back and lifted her hand to tuck a loose strand of hair back behind Anna's ear. She let her thumb run down Anna's face as she did so, pausing at her jawline.

Katherine could feel the urge from her heart to lean forward and place her lips on Anna's. Instead, she gave Anna an apologetic smile and left. Katherine knew she would understand. As soon as she was out of sight, she extracted her phone from her bag and tapped at it frantically.

"Hey," Rebecca answered.

"I told her. I told her everything," Katherine replied with desperation.

"How does it feel?"

"The same. My heart still says go for it, but my head is protecting me. I'm stuck."

Rebecca breathed in steadily. "This is going to hurt, but think about your life before Helena."

Katherine stopped. "What?"

"Knowing now what happened, would you go back in time and stop yourself ever walking into that gallery where you met her? Or would you stand by and watch yourself go in and experience all that heartache again for the amazing times you had with her?"

Katherine knew the answer straight away. She could never wish to not have known Helena just to undo all her own suffering.

"Kat? What would you do?" Rebecca asked firmly.

Tears formed in Katherine's eyes. "I'd watch myself walk straight into that gallery."

"Of course you would. You can't hide behind loss so you can't lose again; it's not how this game is played." Rebecca's voice grew louder and shaky. "If you get knocked down again, I will pick you back up like last time, and I will rebuild you stronger. And I will keep doing it because that's what friends do. But you must keep up your end of that friendship by living life and risking it all. Otherwise, you've learnt nothing from Helena's death, and that would be unforgivable." Rebecca was breathless and panted between sniffs.

Katherine wiped her eyes. The truth hurt; it ached inside her, a mixture of grief and hope.

"You go and get that girl if you want her, but do it knowing that Helena would be cheering you on from the sidelines, telling you to risk it all, because she is."

"But if I hadn't gone into the gallery that night, she would still be alive."

"I thought you were past blaming yourself for the accident?"

Katherine wondered if she really was past blaming herself. She'd accepted that it wasn't her fault someone else decided to drink and then drive into Helena's car, but she felt responsible for them not being safe in bed that night.

As Rebecca had told her over and over, if the hospital had phoned Helena one minute later or earlier to tell her that Katherine had had a heart attack it would have likely affected the outcome. It was a chain of events that only the driver could have prevented, and he was fully to blame.

"Kat, you still there?"

"Sorry, yes. I'm going to sleep on it."

"Okay, love you. Keep me posted and call me — "

"I know, any time. Love you too. Night."

Katherine hung up and crossed the drive to her front door, unsure what her brain would make of everything that had happened in the morning.

CHAPTER 9

*A*nna stretched back against the picnic bench and soaked in the sunshine. Her mind drifted back to the previous night.

She hadn't known how to wake Katherine on her return and couldn't resist stroking her soft face. She had been left drained by her confession and had felt sick since. Knowing that Katherine was carrying around such an immense loss every day, likely scared to open herself up again, pained her.

Anna cringed at the thought of the times she had flirted with her. Now all she wanted was to take away her pain. She wasn't sure how she would ever recover from something like that. Her own problems paled in comparison to Katherine's.

She vowed to keep a distance in future and not flirt with Katherine; it wasn't fair to her. She was sure Katherine had been tempted to kiss her last night but had struggled. She had to be left to make the next move and to be sure of her feelings towards Anna. She couldn't be in any doubt now as to how Anna felt about her, though; Anna felt that her desire to scoop her up in her arms, kiss her, and make everything better for her was inevitably clear.

Trauma of that kind was hard to run from, let alone ever escape. Katherine would no doubt have to learn to live with it, and she was likely learning every day.

A voice pulled her from her thoughts.

"Hey."

Anna sat up and blocked the sun with her hand. "Hi, Carrie."

Carrie joined her on the bench. "They are talking to the investigators, and then Margaret wants to see you. It's typical it happened your first time on call. Was your dad all right on his own?"

"Katherine came over and sat with him."

"Oh, yeah?" Carrie nudged at Anna's side with her elbow.

"What?" Anna tried to contain a smile.

"You and the doc are becoming pretty close."

Anna's mouth betrayed her. "I adore her, Carrie."

"I'm just glad to see you happy. You look so much lighter."

"I feel it. It's nice to have someone looking out for you and caring for you."

Carrie nodded. "Situations like yours can be very lonely and all-consuming."

Two police officers strolled past them and gave them a nod.

"Looks like I'm up." Anna stood and stretched. "See you in a bit."

The meeting room door was already open, so Anna stuck her head around the door. "Hi, Margaret."

Margaret looked up from her position at the end of the long meeting table. "Anna, come in. Close the door please."

Anna took the seat beside her.

"Did the police find out how they broke in?"

Margaret shook her head and dropped her glasses down her nose to look at Anna. "They didn't break in, Anna; the outer gates were left unlocked."

Anna's face fell flat. "But I locked… up." Anna retraced her movements after Katherine had left the abbey the previous afternoon. Her mind scrambled to fill in the blanks. A line etched between her brows. "I'm sure I did." She could visualise closing the gates and putting the lock on, but she had been distracted, her mind full of Katherine and her admittance to being enraptured.

"They examined the combination lock, and there is no sign of it being tampered with. It just appears to have not been clicked in properly. Seems we were the victims of opportunists. Of course, without a crime, there is no insurance payout."

"Shit." Anna put her hand to her mouth. "Sorry."

"It's fine. You must be disappointed."

"Am I going to be fired? I need this job. I love this job."

Margaret breathed in heavily. "At this stage, I don't know. I need to review the results of the investigations with the other trustees before we decide. The site won't be opened until we can get some landscapers to fix the torn-up turf. It's a bit of a health and safety nightmare out there. I suggest you go home for the rest of the day. I'll call you to let you know the outcome as soon as I can."

Anna nodded in agreement and navigated her way back to the bench outside in disbelief. Her chest was tightening, and her head was spinning. Luckily, Carrie was still there.

Carrie rose and crossed the grass to meet her. "Are you all right, Anna? You look like you did after you fainted. You haven't had another episode, have you?"

Anna shook her head and reached out a hand to her. Carrie took it and led her to the bench.

Anna took some deep breaths and closed her eyes, trying to settle the panic she could feel rising inside.

"I... I didn't... lock up properly."

Carrie pushed her lips out and exhaled loudly. "Have they fired you?"

Anna shrugged. "She'll call me."

"Do you want me to run over and get Katherine?"

Anna shook her head. "She'll only fuss."

"Sit for a minute and I'll walk you home."

Anna nodded her agreement.

CHAPTER 10

*K*atherine swept up the vibrating phone from the kitchen island and cleaned under it. She tapped the answer button with her left thumb and tucked the phone between her left shoulder and ear.

"So, how did sleeping on it go?" Rebecca asked instantly.

"I took a sleeping tablet."

"Oh, that bad."

"I just go round in circles, Becks."

"Have you seen her today?"

"No, but I should. Clear the air and all that."

There was a pause on the line.

"Why do you need to clear the air? What exactly happened?"

Katherine stopped cleaning and moved the phone to her right ear.

"As I was leaving, we hugged, and then I…" She wandered over to the patio doors.

"You didn't kiss her?" Rebecca asked, a little too much excitement in her tone.

"No, I couldn't bring myself to."

"Oh." Rebecca paused. "I think that's probably worse than kissing her, isn't it?"

Katherine laughed. "It certainly feels that way."

"You should definitely address that; she's probably wondering what's wrong with her."

"I'll try and catch her between tours this afternoon."

"You do that. Catch me up later, we're being called back in for the verdict," Rebecca replied, distracted.

"Good luck." Katherine hung up and held her phone to her chest. Rebecca was right: leaving Anna hanging had been unforgivable, but she had explained her situation, so surely she would understand her hesitation.

She counted the hours down until Anna would finish her first afternoon tour and likely be on a break. When the time came, Katherine walked across the drive only to notice that the abbey car park was a lot emptier than normal. Where there would normally be twenty cars, there were two.

"Hi, Carrie, I was hoping to catch Anna," she shouted over to Carrie who was just leaving the visitor centre.

Carrie approached her.

"The site has been closed; they sent her home early whilst they decide her fate." Carrie grimaced.

"What do you mean?" Katherine shook her head in bewilderment. "She's not responsible for the break-in surely?"

Carrie pointed to the gates. "She didn't lock them properly. A couple of kids got in with a car and tore the grounds up. It's a bit of a mess back there. Needs a bit of landscaping."

"Are the trustees still here?"

"Yes, Margaret is inside. If you catch up to Anna, try and persuade her to come to the quiz at the pub tonight. She seems to listen to you. I think she could do with a bit of downtime; she was more than a little stressed earlier."

Katherine nodded and walked to the visitor centre. She knew exactly what she needed to do.

Katherine was surprised to see Harry answer the door when she arrived at Anna's house later that day.

"Harry, I was expecting Anna to be home."

"Come in, doc. She's in the garden." He shuffled himself backwards out of the way.

Katherine smirked at his address and entered.

"Go through, she's in a bit of a state."

Katherine made her way through the kitchen to the back door and poked her head out.

Anna was on the phone but, having spotted her, beckoned for Katherine to join her.

The garden was bigger than Katherine had imagined it would be. It would be a nice place to sit out with Harry when she read to him.

"Thank you, Margaret. I'll see you tomorrow." Anna hung up and let out a breath of relief. "I thought I lost my job there for a minute" — she looked to Katherine with her eyebrows raised — "but it seems someone spoke to

Margaret and apologised for distracting me when I was locking up. You weren't even there then."

"No, but I did distract you. I feel responsible; I'm sorry." Katherine moved closer to her.

"None of this is your fault, it's all on me, but thank you for speaking up for me. It did the job. I've been stressing all afternoon trying to work out how we'd survive without my earnings."

"Well, if you feel like celebrating, Carrie was saying something about the pub tonight. Why don't you go? I can come back later and sit with Harry."

"I'm not sure I can ask you to dad-sit two nights in a row."

"Anna, I'm offering. Please go. It will put my mind at rest that you're out enjoying yourself for once."

Anna was silent for a moment, cogs whirring with logistics.

"If you're sure? I do love a quiz. I'll get him to bed, and he can manage to get to the toilet himself, so he shouldn't be any trouble."

"Great. What time do you want me?" Katherine asked.

"Just before eight? I should be back by ten."

Katherine nodded and watched as Anna held on to the table and took a deep breath.

"Are you all right? Carrie said you were in a bit of a state after you found out."

"I nearly had another panic attack."

Katherine walked straight to her and hugged her.

"Honestly, I'm fine now, thanks to you saving my job."

Katherine felt Anna's tense body relax into hers. She could feel the tips of her fingers tensing, calling out to be run through Anna's hair. She loosened her grip on Anna, hoping it would signal they should stop. Anna pulled away and flashed her a smile that made her legs tingle.

Katherine looked at her watch. Although she would see Anna later, if somewhat briefly, she had no desire to be separated until then. What if she wasn't as okay as she made herself out to be? She should stay close for a while, just to make sure.

"It's only four now. You sit here." She manhandled Anna into a garden chair. "Give me ten minutes to go back home and grab some ingredients, and then I'll be back to make dinner."

Anna opened her mouth to speak but closed it again, nodding instead.

Katherine walked to the back door.

"You'll be joining us, won't you?" Anna called out.

"You try and stop me. Now don't move. I'll glue Harry to his chair on my way out."

She returned within the allotted ten minutes to find Harry and Anna still pinned to their chairs. She pulled a shepherd's pie together and popped it into the oven. By the time she checked on them again, they'd both dozed off. She returned to the kitchen to lay the table and prep the veg.

Anna left bang on eight. Katherine watched her as she jogged over the road to the pub. As soon as she closed the front door, Harry appeared on the stairs in his dressing gown.

He grinned like a naughty teenager. "Has she gone?"

"She has."

"Pour me a whisky, will you, doc? It's hidden at the

back of the cupboard beside the sink. Get yourself one too." He shuffled down the last few steps and over to his chair.

Katherine shook her head with a grin. She found the bottle of whisky where instructed and poured a small amount into two glasses, knowing his beaker would smell of it if she'd used that. She made a mental note to clean them up before Anna got back.

"Here." Katherine held the glass in front of him and helped him take a sip.

"Ah, good stuff that."

"Just tell me when you want more."

Harry nodded. "I will, doc."

She rolled her eyes and grinned; it wasn't worth correcting him.

Harry sat back in his chair. "She's very fond of you, you know."

"I know, I'm very fond of her too."

"But…?"

Katherine got the feeling that Harry had come down for "the chat".

"I've lost a lot already," she said. "I'm not sure I'm brave enough to open myself to more."

"Ah, to live is to lose. If you're not losing, then you're not living, and then what's the point of any of it?" he said casually, with a shaky wave of his hand.

Katherine's eyebrows shot up. "Well, that's certainly one way of looking at it."

He gestured to his whisky. Katherine picked it up and held it close to him.

Harry drained the remainder from the glass. "We're

here for a good time, not a long time. You need to make the most of every day before your days run out. Take me, for instance; she keeps me alive and well, but am I living? Am I living the best life I can? I need to be with people my age."

Katherine was surprised to hear Harry's thoughts on the matter. She realised she'd presumed that whatever Anna thought, her father shared that opinion. "I could mention moving you to a home if that's what you'd like? Although you know how she gets about that."

He nodded. "I do. Sometimes I think she needs me more than I need her."

"That wouldn't surprise me. She has agreed that I can take you over to the library and out for short walks or whatever you like. I have a little plan up my sleeve for her later this week, but I'm going to need your help."

"I'd like that." His voice softened. "You're a good sort, Katherine. She'd be lucky to have you in her life; we both would."

Katherine blinked; he'd finally used her name. "I would be the lucky one." She patted him on the hand.

He smiled at her. "I'd best be off to bed, doc. I'll be seeing you soon, I hope."

Katherine got up to assist him.

"It's all right, doc. I can get myself up to bed."

"Night."

Katherine finished her whisky and took the glasses through to the kitchen to clean and put away. She wasn't sure what the problem with a grown man drinking whisky in his own house was, but she was happy to play along with him if he wanted.

A key in the door drew Katherine away from her book. She checked her watch. It was only nine.

Anna opened the door, removing her key from the lock as she entered.

Katherine leaned round onto the back of the sofa. "Back so soon? Surely it can't be over?"

"No, I told them I have a headache," she replied, hanging her jacket up.

Katherine stiffened into doctor mode. She stood and marched over to Anna. "Let me take your pulse. Do you feel like you're going to have another attack?"

Anna held out her hand and faced Katherine.

"Your heart is racing." Katherine placed her hands on Anna's face and looked into her eyes.

"How long have you had a headache?"

"I haven't got a headache. I just told them I had one."

Katherine twisted her head and frowned at her. "Why did you tell them you had a headache if you haven't got one?"

Anna laughed. "Because I didn't want to be there."

"So you do feel unwell?" Katherine felt Anna's forehead, though it felt no warmer than usual.

Anna smirked. "I didn't want to be there because I wanted to be here… with you."

"Oh. But your pulse is racing — oh." Katherine's eyes shot straight to meet Anna's.

Anna nodded slowly.

Katherine's hand found its way down from Anna's

forehead to her cheek. "The last person I kissed was Helena."

"It can stay that way for as long as you want; this is your choice. I'm in this whatever you decide it's going to be."

Katherine took a breath, wavering on a precipice. "You don't give me any choice." She pushed her lips onto Anna's. Her warm mouth invited her in further, down a rabbit hole she knew she would never be able to leave.

Anna wrapped her arms around her and pulled their bodies together. She kissed her with such passion Katherine could feel her knees weaken. She wanted to cry. Helena was drifting away, and although she'd decided it was time, it still hurt.

They finally separated.

"Hmm, Dad had the whisky out, then?"

Katherine recoiled in horror and put her hand to her mouth. "Sorry."

"Don't worry, he thinks I don't know, but he has one every day before I get home from work. Who do you think buys the bottles and puts them there for him? I can't stand the stuff personally, but your lips just improved it somewhat."

Their eyes had trouble meeting, but smiles soon swept over their faces.

"Sorry, I promised myself I wasn't going to flirt with you anymore. I promised I would let you lead," Anna admitted.

"You did, and I am grateful for it," Katherine replied.

"I thought you might not be ready."

"I wasn't earlier today, but your dad said something tonight that made me realise I actually was."

Anna grinned. "Good old Dad. What did he say?"

Katherine hesitated; she didn't quite want to put it the way Harry had. She wanted to put a more positive spin on it. "Something along the lines of 'Every day is for living, and if you aren't living every day, then what's the point of it?'"

Anna pushed her bottom lip out and nodded. "Sounds like Dad. I hope he wasn't any bother."

"Your father is no bother to me; I adore him. Almost as much as I adore his beautiful daughter." Katherine leaned forward and kissed Anna again but didn't linger. "I'm going to leave now. I have some dead-wife emotions to deal with."

Anna gestured to the door. "You deal away. I'll be here if you need me. Say hi to Rebecca for me." She winked.

Katherine smirked at Anna and tapped her lightly on the nose. "Good night, damsel."

Anna tilted her head, her eyes questioning.

"Don't ask."

Katherine left the house and took out her phone, tapping out a message as she joined the high street.

I kissed the damsel! She says hi.

The phone rang within seconds. Katherine answered it.

"Tell me everything, now!"

Katherine chuckled. "I think I summed it up quite clearly in my text."

"How do you feel?"

"Amazing, lighter, excited."

"Fab. I hope I can meet her properly. I'm coming down at the weekend; my case will be over by then."

"Okay, see you then." Katherine hung up and continued her stride towards Abbey house.

For the first time in years, she felt optimistic and excited about the future.

CHAPTER 11

*A*nna stood at the counter, hands on her hips. She was wide awake, full of energy, and the tingle in her chest told her she was happy.

Gloria spotted her and headed to the coffee machine.

"I'll have some of your finest green slime this morning please, Gloria."

Gloria stopped in her tracks and turned to look at her. She grinned and walked to the backroom where she seemed to concoct it. Anna suspected it was so no one could see what she put in it. She returned a few minutes later with the same grin and placed it on the counter.

Anna wondered how long Gloria could go without commenting. She placed the money on the counter and picked up the cup. She got to the door before Gloria caved.

"All right, tell me everything right now, young lady!"

Anna smirked around the straw in her mouth and returned to the counter. "I knew I could break you."

"Come on, out with it."

"There's not much to tell."

"Are you and the other green slime lady green-slime-ing together now?" Gloria did a strange gesture with her finger.

Anna nearly spat out her mouthful of slime. "You seriously need to work on your lesbian metaphors, Gloria, but at least you avoided the word 'scissors'."

"Scissors? What's that got to do with anything?"

"Never mind. We're friends, maybe a little more." She held the straw tightly in her mouth, hoping to disguise her smile, and headed back to the door.

"Well, good luck to you, I say. You need a bit of happiness, darling."

The abbey was a hive of activity when she arrived. Flatbed vans were in the car park with spades leaning against them.

Carrie walked to meet her as she entered through the gate.

"They started at six this morning, both vans laden with fresh turf and eight men. It means we can open today."

"Wow, Margaret sure can pull some things out of the bag."

"The abbey received an anonymous donation yesterday, so I imagine that helped."

"Great," Anna replied, rather subdued at the thought that someone else was paying for her error.

"It was a mistake, Anna, don't beat yourself up. They aren't." Carrie nodded at Margaret and another trustee who were overseeing the men as they finished up.

They perched on the bench and watched as the men packed their vans.

Margaret spotted them and joined them at the bench.

"Morning, ladies. Those chaps have done an excellent job of it. You would never know there had been a problem; they are even coming back to keep the turf watered for us, to make sure it all takes."

Margaret walked back to the visitor centre and waved the workers off in their vans.

Something didn't add up; Margaret was acting too cheery. She hadn't said anything to Anna about the whole palaver, though the repairs must have been a cost the abbey could ill afford.

Anna watched the vans leave; they pulled out of the car park and drove straight onto the drive of Abbey House. She was going to murder Katherine.

Cars began to pile into the car park, though; it was opening time. Anna supposed Katherine would have to wait.

By lunchtime, Anna felt calmer. She was still annoyed at Katherine, though, and intended to have it out with her. It was probably best to get these things aired early on in a relationship. Katherine was rich, and Anna was poor; she needed Katherine to know that she was quite capable of providing for herself and fighting her own battles.

Anna grasped the partially naked knocker. She pushed images of what Katherine would look like partially clad to the back of her mind and banged the knocker.

Katherine opened the door. She had her hair tied up and her glasses on, though she removed them to get a better look at who was on the doorstep.

"Anna, what a nice surprise. I've just finished my surgery for the day." She held the door open wide and gestured her in.

Anna passed her and entered the hallway. This was going to be difficult enough without Katherine looking all sexy. She wondered if she could say everything she needed to without actually looking at her. Unlikely.

She followed Katherine through to the kitchen.

"What were your gardeners doing at the abbey this morning?"

"I believe they were repairing the lawns."

"I know what they were doing there, Katherine. I meant what were *they* doing *there*?"

"You mean why were they there."

Anna put her hands on her hips and glared at Katherine.

"Oh." Katherine pursed her lips. "I lent them my gardeners so you could open today."

Anna raised her eyebrows. "Like you only lent them a donation too?"

Katherine frowned. "How did you know that was me?"

Anna twisted her lips and tilted her head.

"Oh, you didn't." Katherine looked down.

"No, but it appears I made a very good guess. I don't need you to fix my problems. Putting in a word for me was welcome, but this is tantamount to bribery."

"What?" Katherine's head shot straight back up.

"You asked them to not fire me, and then you offer them a donation and then send your gardeners over to repair the damage. No doubt at your expense as well."

Katherine pulled her bottom lip in and bit it. "Sorry, I overstepped. I see that now, but I couldn't stand by and watch you lose your job."

"I know. But it wasn't your place to fix it either."

"If it wasn't for me being there, it wouldn't have happened."

"I invited you if you recall."

"Yes, but I distracted you. Don't deny it or I will be wounded. At my age, the thought of distracting younger women is what gets me through the day."

Anna's eyes narrowed. "Feel free to splash your cash about, but please don't do it on my behalf or for my future benefit. Clear?"

"Clear." Katherine pulled her lips tightly together and nodded firmly.

"I don't feel like I deserve my job now."

"You do deserve it." Katherine moved slowly towards her. "You're the most knowledgeable, most beautiful tour guide I ever beheld." Katherine reached forward and tucked her hand around the back of Anna's neck. Her hand was soft and warm and welcome.

"I'm glad to see that beauty is on the top of the list of requirements for tour guides these days."

Katherine applied a light pressure to the back of Anna's neck, guiding her forward to meet her mouth. Anna's body weakened at the touch of their lips. Katherine was more intense than the first time they had kissed. Anna felt herself leading then, even though Katherine had instigated it. This time, Katherine was very much in control. Her hand worked its way up to the back of Anna's head; her nails clawed lightly into her scalp before she grasped a handful of Anna's hair and pulled it down to raise Anna's chin. Anna groaned as Katherine's mouth found its way to her neck and her hand squeezed her breast.

Anna wanted to reciprocate but found herself unable to move. She was completely under Katherine's control.

"We're all alone," Katherine whispered as her mouth kissed its way back to Anna's.

"We are, but sadly I have to get back."

Katherine released her slowly.

"I need to give a good impression after this week's mishap, and if I stay here any longer, I get the feeling I will be missing my afternoon tour."

"Well, we can't have that, and it also reminds me that I need to be somewhere this afternoon."

"Anywhere interesting?" Anna asked.

Katherine narrowed her eyes at Anna. "There is nowhere more interesting."

"One more thing before I go."

Before Katherine could speak, Anna pounced on her, pushing her back against a kitchen cupboard, kissing her lips as hard as she could. Both her hands grabbed Katherine's bottom, causing her to let out a soft moan which Anna took as consent to carry on. Anna wanted to feel every part of Katherine. She released her grasp on her bottom and filled her hands with Katherine's breasts. Katherine groaned again as Anna caressed them and turned her head to one side, inviting Anna's mouth down to her neck and chest.

Anna suddenly stepped back and let out a long breath.

Katherine panted and smiled at her.

"I'm going now." Anna pointed to the door and backed up. "I better let myself out."

Katherine blew her a kiss as she left.

CHAPTER 12

*I*t had taken Katherine a good fifteen minutes to revive herself after her time with Anna. She looked at her watch and realised she needed to get her skates on if her plan was to come together in time.

She was breathless by the time she arrived to collect Harry and was surprised to find him ready and waiting with his shoes on, although with his laces untied.

"As promised, a new mode of transport for you." She led him out to the front garden and showed him a wheelchair.

"Great, doc. Let's get going."

Katherine locked up and pushed him down the high street to the abbey. She pushed him straight past the visitor centre; one of the benefits of a lifetime pass was that you could take someone else in with you for free. They made their way to the tour point where Anna was already waiting.

"Look, Anna," Harry crowed. "I've got myself a new set of wheels and found myself a rather pretty chauffeur!"

"What are you two doing here?" Anna leaned down to kiss her dad.

"Do I get one of those?" Katherine turned her head and presented her cheek to Anna.

Anna turned Katherine's head to face her and kissed her square on the lips.

"Even better." Katherine blushed.

"That's for getting him into one of those." Anna nodded at the wheelchair. "He's always refused before."

"Harry wanted to see your tour, so I thought it might be the solution."

"I wondered what you were up to, and you were right; there is nowhere more interesting to be, at least in Nunswick."

Anna's tour was even better than Katherine remembered from the walkthrough. Harry was entranced, just like everyone else. It was nice to watch people's faces and see how they responded to Anna, rather than listening intently to what Anna was saying.

At the end of the tour, Katherine and Harry watched in awe as each visitor personally thanked Anna.

"The doc was right: you are brilliant," Harry said when they were finally alone.

Anna blushed. "Go on, get the old man home."

"Harry is coming back to mine," Katherine informed her.

"Are you abducting my father?"

"No, you're more than welcome to join. Actually I'm going to have to insist."

"There's that bossy doctor again."

Katherine winked at her. "You like her, don't you?"

"I might." Anna's face twisted around a smile. "I'll pop home for a shower and change first."

"Okay, we're having a cinema night, so wear something comfy. I'll have dinner ready."

Anna exhaled. "Are you even real?"

Katherine leaned forward and kissed Anna firmly on the lips. "Real enough."

"Come on, you two, stop flirting," Harry said. "There's only so much I can listen to, especially if one of them is my daughter."

"Dad!"

"Come on then." Katherine pushed the wheelchair along the path. "See you later, Anna."

She nodded and flashed a smile at Margaret as they passed her on the path. She hoped she wouldn't stop her to thank her; she had been quite insistent on the donation and repairs being anonymous. Luckily, she seemed distracted and only managed half a smile.

Harry was well into his first war film by the time the knocker resounded through the house.

Katherine opened the door only to be met by a bunch of flowers. Anna followed behind them.

"Just something to say thanks again for everything you are doing for us."

"You shouldn't have, but they are beautiful. Thank you." Katherine kissed her on the cheek. "Come through to the kitchen. Dinner is nearly ready."

Anna leaned over the back of Harry's chair. "You okay, Dad?"

"Great, love. This film is amazing. I can hear

everything from all around me; bombs are coming from everywhere!"

She kissed him on the head and made her way into the kitchen.

"You're spoiling him with your big television and surround sound. He'll never want to leave."

Katherine closed the doors between them and the sitting room. "Speaking of which, I know we have sort of discussed this before, but have you thought any more about a care home? Perhaps you should speak to your father about it, see what he thinks?"

Anna took a seat on a stool at the island and put her head in her hands. "He'll only feel obliged to go if I mention it. You know we'll lose the house to?"

Katherine took a seat beside her, relieved that Anna hadn't immediately flown off the handle. "I suspected that might be the case."

"I rang them. They said if he meets the requirements for a care home, then I'd have to give it up. I grew up there. Mum is there."

Katherine placed a hand on her knee and squeezed it.

"I think for the moment he's better with me."

Katherine stared into Anna's glossy eyes. She placed her hands on her face and wiped under them. "No tears today, except for the men on the battlefields." She leaned forward and kissed her. "Come on, dinner won't serve itself. Do you want to get us a drink?" Katherine pointed to the fridge.

"Champagne again?" Anna asked, opening the fridge to find two bottles in the door.

"You bet. I'm sort of celebrating."

Anna gave her a questioning look and withdrew a bottle.

"It's been a whole day since I picked up the hottest lesbian in the village, and I've made out with her twice since."

Anna grinned. "That's strange. I'm celebrating that too."

After dinner, they were on to the second movie, *Dunkirk*, chosen by Harry.

Anna lay wrapped in Katherine's arms along the largest sofa.

"I wish we could stay like this forever," Katherine whispered into her ear.

"Me too."

"Are you free Saturday? I have plans for you both, a little road trip."

"I am now."

Katherine kissed Anna's head and inhaled the honey scent from her hair. She felt her attraction to the beautiful tour guide was fast turning in to something more — she was falling in love. A pang of guilt hit her in the stomach as her thoughts turned to Helena. She turned her attention to the movie and pushed the thoughts aside.

CHAPTER 13

a car horn tooted outside.

Anna emerged from the kitchen with a shoulder bag. "Come on, Dad, that will be Katherine."

"I just need some help with these darn laces."

Anna opened the front door in case Katherine came and then knelt on the floor in front of Harry.

On cue, Katherine popped her head around the door. "All ready?"

"Nearly. Do you want to grab his wheelchair?"

Katherine spotted the chair parked behind the sofa and lifted it. "Shall I see you outside?"

"Yes, won't be a minute." Anna hoped more than believed that. "Have you been to the toilet, Dad?"

"Yes, I've been, don't make a fuss."

Anna helped Harry up and offered him her arm. She was relieved that he was keen to go wherever it was they were going. It was Katherine's secret, though Anna had been reassured there were ample toilet facilities and paths for Harry's needs. All she knew was that Katherine would collect them at eleven and she was bringing a picnic.

Anna secured Harry in the back seat and jumped into the front seat of Katherine's Porsche Cayenne.

"Any clues as to where we are going in your exceptionally smart car? I'm glad I had a shower this morning," she teased. "I wouldn't want to dirty it."

"Nope," their driver said. "No questions please."

Katherine opened the panoramic sunroof and pushed another button. A netting appeared across the opening and blocked the sun.

"I think this is the poshest car I've ever been in."

They drove for what Anna calculated must have only been a few miles. She recognised the route and took a guess where they were heading but didn't let on. She didn't want to spoil Katherine's surprise.

She snuck a sideways glance at Katherine as she drove and watched her hair as it bounced lightly with the car. Her large sunglasses covered a lot of her face, but her bright red lips called to her. Her body ached to be alone with Katherine. Things had already got heated between them several times, and it was clear it was just a matter of time and opportunity before they went further.

"It's rude to stare," Katherine said, eyes still fixed on the road ahead.

Anna smirked at being caught and turned her gaze to the window to admire the passing countryside.

Despite knowing where they were going, she still felt a slight somersault of excitement in her stomach as they pulled into the car park of Halsey Castle. The place held so many happy memories for her. Often memories filled with lost loved ones would then become unhappy memories, and Anna hoped that wouldn't be the case today. It was time to make more happy memories instead.

The castle was just a ruin, located on top of the highest of a group of hills that overlooked the Nunswick Valley. It was your typical tourist attraction with a lake, gift shop, and cafe.

"Shall we take a wander around the castle before lunch?" Katherine suggested as they exited the car.

Harry eased himself into his chair. "You can see if all your old hiding places are still there. Though don't expect me to come and find you now."

Anna squeezed his shoulder. It was going to bring a lot of memories back for her dad too. She didn't think he'd been back since she was little either. It was a place they would go to every few weeks when she was very small. As she grew older and did her own thing, the castle became just a memory.

As they walked around, she spotted all the little nooks and crannies that she would squeeze herself into, the place she tore her new jeans and was told off by her mum. She felt a pang of guilt that they hadn't returned in so long.

Once they had finished looking around inside the castle walls, they joined the path and walked the route around the outside.

Anna wiped her brow. Pushing a wheelchair in the heat of the day was hard work.

"Do you want me to take over for a bit?" Katherine asked.

"Do you mind? I'm exhausted."

"Not at all." Katherine took her place behind the wheelchair.

Anna walked a little ahead and stretched.

"Hold on, Harry," Katherine shouted and ducked down to put her full weight behind the wheelchair.

Anna turned to see Katherine and Harry charging after her in the wheelchair. She took off along the path.

"Faster," Harry shouted.

Anna ran out of breath and collapsed onto a bench. "You always caught me."

"Now we're both here to catch you." Katherine winked at Anna.

Anna felt warmth rush to her face.

Katherine parked Harry beside Anna. "I'll run back to the car and collect the picnic. You two wait here."

"I'm not going anywhere, doc." He waited until Katherine was far enough away and then nudged Anna. "Reckon you've got yourself a good one there." Harry nodded after Katherine.

Anna watched her as she strolled towards the car park. "I know, Dad. I know."

Katherine reappeared a few minutes later, a walking cliche with her large straw hat, summer dress blowing lightly in the wind, sunglasses, and wicker picnic basket. She looked like a movie star walking on to set. For someone with so much tragedy to bear, she owned her space, or at least did a good job of looking like she did.

They found a shady spot under a tree near the lake and parked Harry beside the picnic basket. Katherine and Anna lay on either side of the spread Katherine had put together. She'd kept it traditional with sausage rolls, scotch eggs, pork pies, sandwiches, and of course ginger beer, all of which was enthusiastically consumed by everyone.

Anna admired Katherine as she arched back into the afternoon sun. She'd organised everything so perfectly to ensure they would have the best day out. Part of her felt she was falling madly in love with her, Jessica now a distant memory. The two women were at complete opposite ends of the spectrum. Katherine was classy, educated, wealthy. Jessica was a party girl; she could dance and drink but do little else.

"Shall we feed the ducks before we fall asleep?" Katherine suggested as she stretched.

"I think we've eaten everything."

"Not these." Katherine pulled out a bag of pellets from the picnic basket.

"You have special duck food?"

"Of course. You shouldn't feed bread to ducks. There's no nutrition in it." Katherine got to her feet and offered a hand to Anna.

"You young'uns go. I'll watch from here."

Katherine pulled Anna up. "Your daughter may be a young'un, Harry, but I'm forty-nine!"

"I'm hardly far behind you!"

Anna realised they were still holding hands. She squeezed it and Katherine reciprocated.

As they made their way to the lake, Anna couldn't think of a time when she'd felt happier. Physically and mentally she felt calmer and more rested than she had done in months. Everything was going fantastically at work, her guidebook was coming along slowly, and she had an exceedingly beautiful woman in the palm of her hand. Literally.

Children paddled in the shallow part at the far end of the lake by the playground, forcing all the wildlife to their end. They were soon surrounded by ducks, all fighting over the pellets.

"Rebecca is coming tomorrow for Sunday lunch. Would you and Harry come? I'd like you to meet her properly."

"No fainting then?" Anna grinned as she threw a handful of pellets in.

"No fainting."

"I'd love to, and I'm sure Dad won't say no as long as he can watch the Formula One on your television."

"I'm sure we can arrange that."

Anna looked around and spotted a brightly coloured cart in the distance. "Fancy an ice cream? My treat this time?"

"I won't say no."

CHAPTER 14

*a*nna grasped at the partially clad lady knocker yet again, pushing the same thoughts as always to the back of her mind. The door was answered by Rebecca.

"Anna, nice to see you again. Harry, it's nice to meet you. Come on in. Kat's in the kitchen."

Kat! A pang of jealousy shot through Anna. She wanted to be the one to call her Kat.

Anna delivered Harry to his usual seat in front of the television and helped him find the correct channel. Rebecca was working away on a laptop on the kitchen island when she entered, a glass of champagne next to her. Katherine was clearly dressed up under her apron. Her short skirt and stockinged legs made Anna suck in her breath, drawing her thoughts back to the last time she'd been in the kitchen and caressed parts of Katherine she'd once dreamed of. She wished Rebecca wasn't there so she could close the doors and do it all over again.

"Becks, can you do Anna a glass?"

"Oh, sure." Rebecca shot up.

Becks! They had pet names for each other; maybe they weren't just good friends, or at least in the past hadn't been. She felt jealous of their closeness.

Katherine approached her, taking her breath away again as she grew nearer. When she wrapped her arms around her and kissed her, slipping her tongue into her mouth, Anna almost buckled. She tasted of champagne.

Rebecca filled a glass with champagne and passed it to Anna.

Katherine returned to pottering around the kitchen, and Anna took a seat beside Rebecca at the island.

"Harry, can I get you anything?" Katherine called through to the sitting room.

"I'm all right at the minute, doc. Thanks."

Rebecca hit a button on her laptop and then shut the lid. She turned to Anna as she took a sip from her glass.

"No tours this weekend, Anna?"

"I've been training two new tour guides. This is their first weekend going it alone."

"You were the only tour guide before, am I right?"

"Yes, just me. My boss covers when I'm not there."

"With your dad to care for too. No wonder you fainted."

"Yes, it was getting a bit much, but I needed to make a good impression when I first started. It seems to have paid off. I should have weekends completely free now, well, to spend a bit more time with Dad."

Katherine coughed loudly.

Anna smirked. "And Katherine, of course. So, how long have you two been friends?" Anna thought it might be a good time to extract information about their friendship.

Katherine and Rebecca looked at each other and grinned. Anna's heart sank. An in-joke, she regretted asking.

"Rebecca pulled me out of the backwater at Cambridge."

"She was hopelessly drunk and fell out of the punt. I was on the punt behind, working, I might add."

"She dragged me on to her punt and got me back to shore. Her digs weren't far away, so she let me clean myself up. We got to chatting and hit it off," Katherine said.

"We shared a house in our remaining years."

"Until you left me stranded in Cambridge all alone because you were called to the bar."

"You were never alone, Katherine." Rebecca winked at Anna.

Anna fidgeted in her seat. She was sure Katherine had a past, but it wasn't something she wanted to hear about so soon or from someone else.

Katherine seemed to sense the distress rising in Anna and walked around behind her, placing her arms over her shoulders, and pulling her back to rest against her.

"Let's not rake over the past, Rebecca, or I may have to mention all your conquests, and we simply don't have time to cover that many men!"

"That was the best bit sharing a house with a lesbian, Anna: we were never in competition for the same people."

Anna felt some relief at the confirmation that Rebecca

was straight and her relationship with Katherine was purely platonic.

A buzzer went off.

"Right, folks, that's lunch!"

Katherine insisted on clearing up after lunch and would take no assistance. Anna resettled her dad into his chair, where he was soon joined by Virginia. She returned to the kitchen and lingered awkwardly, not sure where to put herself. "Are you sure I can't help?"

Katherine approached her and planted a kiss on her forehead. "Go chat with Rebecca. I want you two to get to know each other."

Anna did as instructed and collapsed onto a patio chair in the sunshine next to Rebecca. She wasn't sure how they were going to get to know each other; they seemed to be very different people with little in common. She found Rebecca intimidating. Then again, she had found Katherine intimidating to start, and that soon wore off.

Rebecca picked up the champagne bottle and gestured with it to Anna.

Anna shook her head. "I have to look out for Dad. Can't have the wobbly leading the wobbly."

Rebecca nodded her understanding.

Dishes banging drew Anna's attention to the kitchen. "She's in her element."

"She likes a full house. It stops her thinking about things."

Anna wasn't sure how to respond. Was Rebecca trying to initiate a conversation with her about Katherine's past? It wasn't exactly an appropriate topic, considering

Katherine wasn't there. She decided to try a change of subject.

"So you two have been friends for some time then."

"Yes, I've been with her through the good and the bad times."

The change of tack clearly hadn't worked, so Anna decided to face it head-on. "I don't intend to hurt her, you know."

Rebecca dropped her sunglasses down her nose a fraction and peered over them at Anna. "There's no suggestion you would intend on doing anything. Usually people don't set out with that intention."

"I understand any misgivings you might have about Katherine entering a relationship after... what happened."

"What happened? You have no idea what happened." Rebecca raised her voice a little and deepened her tone. "Katherine needed a full rebuild, physical, mental, emotional, you name it. She thought the only way to protect herself was to withdraw from everything. I became her last contact with the real world. I pulled her back from the brink when I thought she might do something stupid. Cradled her night after night as she cried herself to sleep. Held her in the day as she screamed that she wanted to die so she could be with Helena and the baby."

Anna felt tears forming in her eyes and dropped her sunglasses from her head to cover them.

"Anyway." Rebecca smiled, calm again. "There are no misgivings. I actively encouraged Katherine to make new friends and put herself back out there. It's what any good friend should do. It doesn't mean they won't worry when they see their friend putting their heart back on their sleeve, especially when one has invested so much in repairing that heart."

Anna could understand her outburst. Rebecca must have known Katherine had opened up to her, but she wanted to ensure Anna knew the real depth of Katherine's despair. But anger rose in her nonetheless; she knew what was at stake, and she certainly hadn't gone into it for a bit of fun.

"I'm serious about Katherine; this isn't some dalliance for me. I may not have been there to witness her breakdown, but I'm sure as hell going to be there to witness her happiness after, and I'm going to ensure I'm the cause of it because I — "

The patio door opened behind them. Anna fell into silence.

"Becks, I hope you've been playing nicely?" Katherine asked as she stepped out.

Rebecca flashed her a smile in return.

Anna stood. She needed a moment away to clear her head. "Here, have my chair. I'd best check on Dad."

Katherine stopped her as she passed. "Don't mind Becks; she's very protective of me," she whispered in her ear before placing a kiss on her cheek.

As they watched *The Bridge on the River Kwai*, one of her father's favourites, Anna lay tucked into Katherine, her head resting on her chest, lifting with every breath, but she struggled to get the conversation with Rebecca out of her mind. Surely it must have been some sort of test. The sound of light tapping on a keyboard came from the kitchen. Rebecca had begged off from watching the film, claiming a busy week ahead at work and a dislike for war movies.

Anna had an idea.

"I'm just going to get a glass of water." She pulled herself away from Katherine, which gave her a whiff of her perfume.

"I can go if you want?"

"No, it's fine. I don't mind."

She needed to clear the air with Rebecca; the last thing she wanted was for her to put doubts in Katherine's mind because she didn't like her girlfriend.

"You passed, if that's what you're worried about," Rebecca said as soon as Anna had closed the door.

Anna rolled her eyes as she took a glass from the cupboard. How on earth did she know what she had been thinking? She was now on the back foot.

"You were saying something before Kat came out earlier," Rebecca continued.

Anna stared out the kitchen window as water filled her glass. "I love her."

"Have you told her that?" Rebecca asked, completely unfazed by Anna's declaration.

"Of course not. It's far too soon." Anna took a sip of water and turned to face Rebecca.

Rebecca continued to type on her laptop, eyes still fixed on it. "Far too soon to express but not to feel."

Anna observed her. "Something like that."

Rebecca finally looked up from her laptop. "I've never really understood that notion."

Anna approached the other side of the island and took Rebecca in as she stared back at her.

"Look, Anna, I'm sorry if I'm a bit abrupt about going about things. I love her too; I just want the best for her, and who knows? That might just turn out to be you. I hope it does."

"I'm glad you approve," Anna replied and returned to the warmth of Katherine.

Afternoon yawns led to talk of leaving. Anna regretted not bringing the wheelchair. She'd felt her dad could use the walk to Katherine's but hadn't considered being tired and very slightly heady from the champagne after.

To Anna's surprise, Rebecca reached out and hugged her. "It was nice to meet you properly, Anna."

"Likewise." Anna hoped she had done enough to convince Rebecca she was worth it.

"Here, Harry, let me assist you out." Rebecca held her arm out, and he took it gratefully.

Katherine placed her hands on either side of Anna's face and kissed her. "Thanks for coming. I hope you liked Becks."

"I'm sure I will — we have just met," Anna reminded her. The jury was still out on that one. "Lunch was lovely. You really are a great cook. I'm looking forward to seeing where else your skills lie?"

Katherine opened her mouth to speak but then bit her bottom lip.

Anna winked at her as she blushed, and then stepped outside. Rebecca stood aside and Anna slowly guided her father down the drive.

CHAPTER 15

atherine topped up the vase on the centre table of the hall. The flowers Rebecca brought her from London were always so fresh. She claimed they were from the Covent Garden flower market, but Katherine knew that was wholesale only. No doubt they were from a gentleman friend who worked there or a client.

"Good morning. Are you off?" Katherine watched as Rebecca descended the stairs with her suitcase.

"Afraid so."

"And the verdict?"

"I like her. She seems completely devoted to her father, which is a good sign, and there's something about her..."

Letters appeared through the letterbox and dropped onto the mat. Katherine picked them up.

"She's feisty," Rebecca concluded. "She won't take any of your crap."

Katherine swatted Rebecca with the letters and sifted

through them. One caught her attention, and she scrabbled to open it. Her face dropped as she read it.

"What is it?" Rebecca asked.

"Shit," was the only reply Katherine could muster.

"Kat?"

Katherine sat on the bottom of the stairs. Her knees had weakened, and she didn't trust them to hold her up.

Rebecca approached her, and Katherine passed her the letter.

"The General Medical Council? What do they want?" Rebecca's eyes whizzed over the contents of the letter.

Katherine dropped her head into her hands.

"But Anna's not your patient. What's their problem with you having a relationship?"

"Patients, family, they're much the same thing to the GMC, and I have actually seen her as a patient."

"And you knew this right… before you…"

Katherine nodded. She had no excuse. It had been drilled into her since medical school: *You must not use your professional position to pursue a sexual or improper emotional relationship with a patient or someone close to them.*

"Why do it then?"

"It was so gradual. I just wanted to help her, to help them. I didn't realise I was falling in love. It wasn't part of the plan, and by the time I knew I was, it was too late; there was no going back. I just had to hope no one would care."

"You tried to build a relationship on a wing and a prayer, knowing it could all crash down?" Rebecca shook her head. "That poor girl, you don't deserve her."

"I know."

"Shit, Kat. Why did you let me encourage you? I thought it was just patients you couldn't have relationships with." Rebecca ferreted in her handbag for her phone and put it to her ear. "Adrian, it's Rebecca Harvey. I have a favour to ask."

Katherine watched Rebecca as she paced the hallway explaining the situation to whoever Adrian was. She eventually hung up and marched to the kitchen.

"Right, that's my friend Adrian, who specialises in this medical grey area sort of thing. He says to send him a copy of the letter right away, and he'll come back with your options. Once you decide, he'll send the response from his office."

Rebecca placed the letter on the kitchen island in a ray of sun and took photographs of it on her phone, tapping furiously at it before placing it down on the marble work surface.

"Now what?" Katherine asked sheepishly.

Rebecca looked at her watch. "We wait."

They sat in silence, waiting for the phone to ring. Occasionally exchanging glances, Katherine could feel Rebecca's disappointment in her. She was disappointed in herself, but she regretted nothing. Her mind raced with choices and outcomes.

The phone rang. Katherine stared at it and took a deep breath.

Rebecca tutted and picked it up.

"Adrian, hang on, let me put you on speaker." Rebecca placed the phone on the work surface between them.

"Hi, Katherine."

"Hi, Adrian, thanks for your time."

"Not a problem. I owe your friend more than one favour."

Rebecca smirked.

"Right, I'll jump straight to your options. One, admit it and throw yourself on the Council's mercy; you will, however, risk erasure from the register. Has there been any sexual activity yet?'

Rebecca looked to Katherine.

"No."

"Well, that may play in your favour, but no doubt there has been intention; the fact it was absent doesn't discount the seriousness of the allegation. Plus, they may assume it anyway even if you deny it; you know what people are like, and these guys are no different. Two, and I don't advocate lying, especially to the GMC, deny everything and hope they don't produce any evidence of your relationship. This is just a preliminary stage, so it may not go any further. With this option, you would, of course, have to prevent any evidence from being acquired, so you would need to sever all future ties to the patient's daughter. If there is no evidence, they should drop the case. If they do have evidence, then you are no worse off than option one except they will likely come down harder on you for lying."

The patient's daughter! Her name was Anna, and she was so much more than just the patient's daughter. It sounded like a book you'd see on the bestseller table at Waterstones.

"It's a confirm-or-deny option, Katherine," Adrian stated.

Katherine rubbed at her hands. "There was no mention of a suspension in the letter, so I can keep practising."

"It's a moral rather than a performance case, and with no other regulatory body involved, they wouldn't look to suspend you without further evidence. Now you have my number. All responses need to go back through me; don't contact them yourself."

"Thank you, Adrian. One last thing."

"Fire away."

"Will the GMC inform Anna of the investigation?"

"Assuming she's been named as the other party, it's a possibility. If all they have is a rumour, then it's unlikely."

"I really, really need to keep my job and this patient."

"It's option two then. Mull it over."

Option two: sever all future ties with the patient's daughter. This hit her like a gut punch. "Thanks, Adrian," Katherine managed to say.

"No problem, and I'll see you soon, Rebecca."

"No doubt, Adrian." Rebecca hung up the phone.

"Are you two…?"

Rebecca grinned. "No, we're just friends. What do you reckon then?"

"I don't know. Either way I lose."

"Wouldn't it be better to throw yourself on their mercy? Is she not worth losing your licence over? It's not like you work to live."

"Of course I would pack it all in for her. I love her, but the most important thing to her is that her father gets the best medical care, and she knows I can give that to him. She doesn't trust anyone else. I have to fight to keep my job for her, for Harry, but I'll have to give her up in exchange."

"Talk it over with her please."

Katherine shook her head. "I can't make her be the one to end our relationship, but she will if I tell her, and quite rightly so. What if she ends up resenting Harry for coming between us? Even if she did choose me over him, which she wouldn't, then she'd be risking my licence to practice and throwing her father at another doctor, and she will never rest easy with that. We just can't be together, and I need to find a way to tell her that makes it a clean break. There's only one way to do that: I'll tell her I took on too much too soon; that I wasn't yet ready for another relationship."

"Any ideas who reported you?"

Katherine genuinely couldn't think of anyone. "Most likely a homophobic gossip."

"I imagine there are a lot of them in a village like this."

A new thought crossed Katherine's mind and soured her stomach. "Shit, her father has his medication review in a few days."

"Better get it done before then. If you're sure, I would strongly urge you to talk to her."

"You don't know her like I do; she's not as strong as she makes out. I'm going to go back to Adrian straight away and tell him to deny it; then if the GMC do inform Anna about the complaint against us, I would have removed the burden of choice between Harry's welfare and being with me."

"Well, I suppose your decision is in some way admirable: you'll happily give up the best thing that has happened to you in a long while just so you can make sure she's not stressing about her father's care."

Katherine hoped if Anna did ever find out that she would see it made sense. She was hopeful they could at least remain friends, as painful as it would be.

CHAPTER 16

*M*onday was a perfect morning, with a beautiful, blue sky stretched out above the abbey. Everyone gathered in the cafe area of the visitor centre awaiting Carrie for their weekly staff meeting.

Anna had spotted one of her new tour guides but couldn't see the other one. She hoped she wasn't going to be late as it would reflect badly on her.

Carrie appeared beside her. "Hey, Anna, just to give you the heads-up, Ellie quit this morning."

Anna shook her head. "What? Why?"

"She said it had all been too nerve-wracking, and she's decided on a new career path."

"Great!" Anna exhaled loudly.

Carrie squished her face. "Are you able to cover the tours? I hate to ask."

"I know. I'm sure I can sort something out. Katherine will help if I ask."

"Things going well between you two then?"

"Better than well." Anna fought back a childish smile.

"Good, I'm glad to see you with a twinkle in your eye."

As Carrie stepped away, Anna's pocket vibrated.

She extracted her phone to see a message from Katherine.

We need to talk. Can you pop in on your way home?

Anna's heart pounded in her chest, and then panic overwhelmed her. It felt like a new sensation after the weeks of calm she'd enjoyed, but within seconds it all felt so familiar. Of course this was too good to be true. She shoved her phone back into her pocket and set about doing some quiet deep breathing.

We need to talk usually meant one thing. Had she done something wrong? Had Rebecca disapproved of her and persuaded Katherine to break things off? As much as Anna tried to push thoughts of Katherine's message to the back of her mind, she couldn't.

The end of the day couldn't have come soon enough. She'd already lost her train of thought on a tour when the back of Abbey House came into view. She nearly cried when Virginia turned up for the afternoon tour and insisted on being carried the whole way around. The visitors had loved every minute of it and had assumed Virginia was part of the tour.

When five o'clock came, she sprinted over to Abbey House.

"Anna, come through."

"Is everything okay? You've got me worried."

Katherine remained silent until they got to the kitchen.

"Will you please tell me what's wrong?" Anna said.

Katherine stopped and looked out over the garden. "I'm… I'm sorry, but I need to stop this."

"Stop? Us?"

Katherine nodded. "Yes, I'm sorry. I've made a mistake. I thought I was ready, but I'm not. I hope you can understand."

Anna furrowed her brow. She waited, hoping Katherine would turn it into a joke. She didn't.

Katherine finally turned to face her. "I'm sorry if I've hurt you. It wasn't my intention."

"Is this Rebecca's doing?"

"Rebecca?" Katherine frowned and shook her head. "Why would you say that?"

"I just get the feeling she doesn't approve of me."

"This has nothing to do with Rebecca. She's an important part of my life, but I can make my own decisions."

Anna felt the need to push the point. "You don't deny she doesn't approve of me."

"She approves of you, more than you could realise."

Anna moved closer to her. "Perhaps we could slow things down a little? Did we rush into playing happy families? Did I do something wrong?"

Katherine shook her head and took a small step towards Anna but stopped.

It's not you, you could never do any wrong. I'm just…"

"Not ready."

Katherine nodded. "I'm sorry."

"Will you stop apologising?"

Anna didn't know what to feel. She was heartbroken, but if Katherine wasn't as ready as she had thought she was, then Anna couldn't be angry at her for that.

"Will you still be Dad's doctor?" She held her breath

for the response, she wasn't sure if she would be able to cope if they had to go to a different doctor.

"Of course I will. I would never let you down on that score. I'm here for you both on a professional level, but that is all."

She silently exhaled in relief. At least she would still get to see Katherine in some capacity, though seeing her and not being with her was going to be hard.

"He has his medication review coming up."

Katherine nodded. "I know you must hate me right now, but this doesn't need to be awkward."

"Will you continue to read to Dad?" She could feel hot tears forming in her eyes.

"I don't think I should, no. I'm sorry."

Anna nodded, tears now rolling from her eyes. "I should go." She didn't want Katherine to see her cry.

"I'm — "

"Sorry. Yes, you said, but it doesn't make it any easier."

She couldn't hold the tears back once she left the house. The potential life she'd dreamed of with Katherine was as firmly shut as the door behind her. During the short walk home, she could only feel numbness and disbelief. She was relieved when she finally put the key in the lock and could hide away on the other side of the door.

"You all right, Dad?"

"Yeah, I'm all right. You?"

"Not really, Dad. Katherine ended it. She said she's not ready. A lot happen in her past, and I guess she needs more time to deal with it."

"Oh, that's a shame." Harry frowned.

"You're telling me."

"There, there, I'm sure things will come right. Is she still going to be my doctor?"

"Yes, you have your medication review in a few days."

"All right, love."

"I'll be upstairs if you need me." Anna raced up the stairs, unable to hold in her disappointment any longer.

CHAPTER 17

$\mathcal{K}$atherine felt the quiet of the house even more keenly since it had been so full at the weekend. Her surgery wasn't due to start until 1:00 p.m. that day. She was dreading it; her first appointment was Harry.

She hadn't seen Anna since she'd broken things off with her. She hoped she wouldn't come but knew she would and should. Having enough knowledge of Anna's routine, she had been careful not to cross paths with her. She'd gone to the library on a different day to normal and completely avoided the tearoom.

She'd spent most of the morning moping around the house doing odd jobs, overseen by Virginia's watchful eye. Every room Anna had been into she could feel her presence. A memory would flash back into her mind of conversations they had there, where they had sat and laughed.

The kitchen was worse, given the memory of the time they had kissed, and Anna had pushed her against the kitchen cabinets. Her stomach tingled every time she thought of it. She knew it would get easier as time went on; the voices would disappear into the walls, as Anna once put it.

Katherine hadn't heard back from Adrian since she'd instructed him to give the council a response. She wasn't sure if it was a good sign or not, but she knew enough of the process to know it could take some weeks, even months.

Desperate for a distraction from Anna and the boredom of home, she decided to head to work early. She looked through the patient names on her appointment list and yawned. Her passion for medicine came from its unpredictable nature and its ability to challenge her; something in abundance in a city hospital. She could feel her love for it slipping away with every case of haemorrhoids and verrucas that came through her office door.

Before long the clock told her it was one o'clock, and she knew she couldn't put it off any longer. It wouldn't be wise to hold Anna up anyway as she may cause a scene. She took a deep breath and opened the door.

She looked out into the busy waiting room and spotted Harry, Anna at his side as always. Something in her manner reminded her of the old Anna, the one she had met at his first appointment. She looked like she had the weight of the world on her shoulders yet again. This time Katherine felt responsible for some of it, and this time she had no way of easing it either.

"Harry Walker."

Anna's eyes shot up from the floor to meet Katherine's. This was going to be harder than she thought.

"Come through." She watched as they took the same seats as before.

Katherine took her seat behind the desk. She decided to avoid addressing Anna for as long as she could.

"Harry, how have you been?"

"Missing your big telly, that's for sure, doc," he replied casually.

Katherine and Anna's eyes met each other's in an instant. Anna turned to her dad.

"She means how have you been managing with the Parkinson's, Dad?"

"Oh, all right, doc, but the tablets you gave me don't seem to be working much these days."

Katherine wanted to ask why he hadn't told her before now but realised it was wholly inappropriate. It also hit home that a line had been crossed and he didn't feel comfortable talking to her as a doctor.

"Well, shall we up the dose a little?"

Harry nodded.

"How are you sleeping at night?"

"Not great, doc."

"He gets up a lot for the toilet," Anna added.

"I'm going to reclassify you as late-stage three now."

"You have to reclassify him to increase the dosage?" Anna asked.

"Well, yes and no. Obviously, I've been monitoring his abilities quite closely over the last few weeks, and there is a change in his range of movements which I think warrants it. I'm also going to give you a sleeping tablet.

Hopefully, it will prevent the number of occasions he gets up in the night."

Anna nodded.

Katherine pulled the two prescriptions off the printer and signed them. "Again, let me know of any problems with the increased dosage. Ensure he takes his medication early in the morning, and it will interfere less with his sleep, though the sleeping tablets are there if you need them."

Katherine held out the prescription slip to Anna. She took the other end. Katherine held her end and looked directly at Anna. "Anything else, please let me know."

She let go and watched as Anna stood up, assisting her dad to his feet.

Katherine held the door open for them. Harry went through ahead of his daughter.

"Are you okay, Anna? You look really stressed." Katherine preferred the word "stressed" to broken, although the latter was more fitting.

"One of my trainees quit, which means an increase in my workload. I find myself alone again."

Katherine pulled her lips to one side and gave Anna a look that said she was sorry. She had nothing to say that wasn't sorry, and she didn't want to upset Anna by repeating it verbally.

Anna nodded back to say she understood. She turned to walk away, but Katherine touched her arm.

"Anna, I hate to mention it again, but please consider a home. It's for his safety, as he is becomingly increasingly unsteady. Better a week too soon than a minute too late. At least talk to him about it."

Anna looked down at her arm.

Katherine withdrew her hand.

"Thank you, doctor." Anna turned and joined Harry.

Katherine closed the door and returned to her seat. It could have gone worse, but after seeing Anna looking stressed again, she couldn't help but worry about her.

Maybe she should just throw in the towel and give up her licence. She had come to realise Anna was someone she could happily grow old with. She didn't really need to work, but she did enjoy helping others. Giving it all up would be a big step. And then there was Harry. He was the most important person in Anna's life, and Anna was the most important person in hers. His health and wellbeing had to come first, and if Anna only entrusted her with that job, then that would be her role to carry out to the best of her abilities.

CHAPTER 18

*A*nna strolled down the high street, too tired to run home to prepare her dad's lunch like she normally would. She knew the only way she was getting through the rest of the day was with coffee, and she needed it sooner rather than later. She crossed the road and headed to the tearoom.

"Coffee please, Gloria," Anna called over as she entered.

"Back on that, are we?"

"Seems so," Anna replied nonchalantly.

"What does the doctor think about that?"

"I don't really care."

"You had a falling-out?"

"Not sure we had a falling-in," Anna muttered.

Gloria eyed her as the coffee filled the cup. "You look *tired* out, love."

Anna tried to stifle a yawn behind her hand. Why did the mere suggestion of being tired always give one the urge to yawn? "I'm trying to finalise a guidebook for the abbey."

"Burning the candle at both ends, are we?" Gloria passed her the coffee. "This will wake you up."

"Thanks." Anna blew on it and took a sip. "We've got a photographer coming tomorrow, so I need to plan the shots we need taken."

Gloria put her hands on her hips. "That all sounds exciting, but don't you go overdoing it."

"As if I would, Gloria."

"Send my love to Harry for me."

"I will. I'm just on my way to sort his lunch." Anna headed for the door.

"And your own, I hope!"

Anna opened the door and turned back to Gloria. "Of course."

Although she was nervous about the photographer's impending arrival, as they would only get one chance to capture what she needed, she was also excited. The guidebook was currently just words, and she was eager to bring it to life with photographs of the abbey. She was desperate to finalise the text but was anxiously awaiting the arrival of some research she had asked for from an old colleague at the National Archives.

She was relieved to hear crunching of envelopes underfoot as she stepped into the house.

"Sorry, love, I meant to pick them up," Harry called over from his chair.

"It's all right, Dad. I'd rather you leave them for me to get. You might never get back up."

Harry chuckled.

Anna pulled the junk mail out and threw it in the bin.

"You been all right, Dad?" Anna tore into the remaining letter as she walked over to him.

"Yeah, I watched some of that Poirot boxset you got me. Could you change the disc for me before you go?"

"Of course." Anna pulled out the letter and instantly realised it wasn't the research she was waiting for.

She only picked out a few words as she scanned it: General Medical Council, misconduct, Dr Atkinson. Numbness infused her body, and she perched on the arm of the sofa to read the letter more properly. She could ascertain that Katherine had been reported for misconduct. There was a paragraph about inappropriate relationships with patients and their families and one that stated that the council required a written response as soon as possible.

Katherine breaking it off with her was now starting to make a lot of sense. She was trying to save her career, and Anna had meant nothing to her. Her heart rate quickened; she could feel it pulsing in her neck.

"Everything all right, love?"

"Yeah, fine." Anna shoved the letter back in the envelope, folded it, and shoved it into her back pocket. "I'll get your lunch sorted, and then I've got to nip somewhere before I head back to work."

She couldn't wait until after work. She needed to have it out with Katherine as soon as possible and ascertain what the hell she had been thinking ever pursuing a relationship with her when the letter quite clearly stated it was outside the GMC rules.

All her respect for Katherine had abandoned her. She felt used, like Katherine had picked her up for a few weeks to play with and then just thrown her in the corner when she got caught playing with the wrong toy.

Unable to bring herself to knock using the naked-lady knocker, Anna banged hard on the door itself. Too hard. "Shit." She cradled her hand in the other and winced in pain.

Katherine opened the door and, spotting her, did a quick check around. "Anna? You shouldn't be here."

Anna barged her way past Katherine and into the house.

"Why shouldn't I be here, Katherine? Are you afraid someone will see us?"

Katherine shot a look at Anna but remained silent.

Anna waved the letter at her. "So you knew the GMC were investigating us? Does that have something to do with the space you needed? Hm?"

Katherine lowered her head and took a deep breath before answering. "Come through."

She walked into the sitting room, followed closely by Anna.

"You give me some bullshit about not being ready to get close to me when really you were trying to save your career." Anna couldn't help herself; all her bottled-up disappointment over their split boiled over, and she let it rip. "Did I mean nothing to you?"

Katherine turned sharply to face Anna; her face flushed. "Do you really think so little of me that you could believe that to be true?"

They stood glaring daggers at each from across the sitting room.

"Why didn't you tell me? I thought we were sharing."

"Yes, but not burdening." Katherine took a seat at one end of a sofa. "Saving my career was farthest from my mind; being able to be able to remain Harry's doctor was at the forefront. I'm sorry you can't see that. I know how important it is to you."

Anna let out a deep breath, and sat at the other end of the sofa. "You should have spoken to me. We could have found a way."

"Involving you would have put you in an impossible position."

Anna couldn't understand how and shook her head.

"I wasn't going to put you in a position where you had to choose between me and your father. You've already given up so much to look after Harry; you've worked yourself into the ground to provide for him. I couldn't have you resent him for coming between us, and if I'm being honest, I couldn't face being rejected by you, so the only choice I had was to break it off."

"Well, a masterly plan, I'll give you that, but you didn't account for one thing."

Katherine looked at her and shook her head.

"I would have chosen you."

"You say that now. You know I would have had to pass Harry on to another doctor."

"Yes, I get that, but you taught me to trust. But at the first test of that trust, you didn't trust *me* to be brave or even let me decide or… have the decency to discuss it with me. I would have chosen you because then he wouldn't have been your patient, but he would have been your father too. We would have been a team. I trusted you as Katherine, not your position as Dr Atkinson. Perhaps it's you who has the trust issues, not me."

The room fell silent.

Katherine lowered her head. "I guess I underestimated the depth of your feelings for me."

"Seems that way, doesn't it? You seem to have underestimated a lot of things."

"It's not a good sign that they've written to you. Can I ask what your letter said?"

"They've asked for a response regarding a report of misconduct."

"If you don't back up my version of events and deny the allegations, then they will know I've lied, and it will be game over for my license."

Anna squeezed her fist; the letter buckled. "We did nothing wrong. Surely they can see that we're consenting adults?'

"I used my professional position to pursue a relationship with someone close to my patient. It goes against good medical practice. I shouldn't have kissed you that night."

Anna wanted to pull her hair out. "I can't believe my life is being dictated to me by a group of people that have no business in it."

Katherine bit her lip. "What will you do?"

"I'll write to them and deny the best thing that has happened to me. What other choice have you left me with?"

Anna felt the conversation was probably at its end, but

one thing still niggled at her. "It was a complete lie then, that you weren't ready?"

"I'm sorry. I didn't want to lie to you. I just needed it to be a clean break. I should have listened to Rebecca."

"Rebecca?"

"She said I should talk it over with you."

Anna chuckled. "Rebecca obviously has more sense than you."

"Maybe she knew better than I did how you really felt about me."

"Perhaps." Anna scolded herself. She'd opened her heart to Rebecca when all along she should have said it all to Katherine instead. "Well, I don't think there is much more to say."

Katherine met Anna's gaze and gave a dejected nod. "We should avoid further contact if we can, beyond medical appointments."

"Consider it done." Anna turned and left the room. Katherine looked as if she was about to break down in tears and she didn't know how to handle it if she did. She made sure to shut the front door as hard as possible; the brass knocker made a loud bang behind her. She knew it was childish, but she felt so tired and emotional she hadn't been able to help herself.

CHAPTER 19

atherine rinsed her hair off under the warm spray of the shower. It had been a long day and turned into a long night. Her attempt to preoccupy herself with the coving in one of the front bedrooms had distracted her, but also tired her out. It had been a few weeks since she had last spoken to Anna, and she was feeling every minute of it.

She turned the shower off and heard the buzzing of her phone on the bedside table. She grabbed her towel and extracted herself from the shower, tiptoeing through to the bedroom. She hit the green button as soon as she could reach it.

"Becks, hang on, let me just put you on speaker." She placed the phone on the bed and dried herself with the towel.

"Hey, we won the case!" Rebecca squealed.

Katherine could barely make her out with the background noise. "I'm so pleased for you, Becks; you must be so relieved."

"I cannot begin to tell you."

"Are you at the pub by any chance?"

"Of course! A few of us have decided to go away for a few days' skiing."

"Great, you deserve a break."

"So, how are things with you? How did the damsel take it?"

"It's hell, Becks."

"You should have rung me."

"I knew you were busy the last few days with the case. I didn't want to distract you with my problems again."

"Never too busy for you, Kat."

"She was upset of course but seemed to understand, but then the bloody General Medical Council wrote to her asking for a response to the allegation."

"So she knows your lame-arse excuse that you weren't ready for a relationship was a lie." Katherine could hear Rebecca sucking in air through her teeth.

"Indeed, and she said she would have chosen me. We would have been a team looking after her father, and it was me she trusted, not the fact that I was a doctor."

"Eek. Is this where I don't mention that I told you so?"

"It's done now, Becks. I did it for the right reason. Even if I'd spoken to her and she'd persuaded me that I should fall on the GMC's mercy, I could have lost my job."

"I thought you didn't care about that."

"Becks, I'm trying to convince myself that I made the right decision here. You're not helping."

"I can't say you did, but you made the decision based on what you had to work with, and you're going to have to suck that up. What have you been up to today?"

Katherine wandered out of the room and into another bedroom.

"You'll be pleased to know the ceiling mouldings came back for your room. They look great. I've been painting them." Katherine switched to Facetime and showed Rebecca the painted strips.

"My lush weekend pad is becoming lusher."

A flash of blue light caught Katherine's attention; she pressed her nose against the window.

"Kat, you still there?"

"Sorry, there's an ambulance leaving the village."

"So?"

"It could be one of my patients."

Katherine ran back to her bedroom and scrabbled to get dressed, dropping her phone in the process. A muffled sound came from it.

Katherine picked it up from the floor. "I'll call you back later." She pushed the "End Call" button and stuffed the phone into the trousers she'd just got on.

She leapt through the front door within two minutes and ran down the road.

She stopped suddenly when she saw a figure at Anna's front door but realised it wasn't her. Her heart thumped so hard in her chest she could barely get her words out.

"Excuse me… has something happened… to Anna or Harry?"

The woman jumped and tightened her dressing gown around her. "Yes, I'm just locking up. Had to clean up a bit of blood, didn't want her coming home to it."

Katherine put her hand to her chest. "Please can you just tell me what happened?"

"Oh, Harry took a tumble down the stairs."

Katherine tried not to picture Harry losing his balance on the stairwell. She willed him to be all right. In a way she was relieved; at least the ambulance was an indication of life.

"How was Anna?"

"Well, who can say," the woman replied as she removed the key from the lock.

Katherine fidgeted on the spot.

"She came out breathing into a paper bag."

"Thank you, I'll head up to the hospital now."

"Tell her I've locked up. I'm from next door."

Katherine nodded and ran back to her house. Within minutes she was speeding out of Nunswick, through the darkness of the valley. Her eyes moistened at the thought of Harry injured or worse, and Anna all alone. She pushed the accelerator harder, determined to be with her as quickly as possible, and wiped her eyes. She had the advantage that nighttime brought: you could see any headlights coming long before the car, but only if you weren't blinded by tears.

A movement in the hedgerow caught her eye. A deer shot out, and she slammed on the brake, stopping just in front of it. The animal stared at her for a moment before disappearing slowly into the wood. Katherine exhaled hard. She checked her rearview mirror and then rested her head on the steering wheel. An image of Helena came to mind. Had she been speeding to get to the hospital too? Katherine swallowed hard and pushed the thought away. She needed to get to the hospital as safely as possible. She turned the radio on, pressed her preset button for Classic FM, and continued her journey.

Thankfully there was no problem finding parking at the Accident & Emergency department in Hardwick. Katherine ran into the reception and approached the desk. "I'm Dr Atkinson. You have my patient here, Harry Walker?"

"He's just come in. They are assessing him. Do you know his daughter? She's in a bit of a state."

"Yes, I've met her in my surgery. Can I see her?" Katherine tried to limit the level of concern in her voice. *Stay professional.*

"I'll ring the nurse to come and get you."

Katherine paced the waiting area; she desperately wanted to get to Anna.

A nurse appeared through a pair of double doors and looked at Katherine. "Harry Walker?"

Katherine nodded in reply and followed her down a corridor.

"How is Mr Walker?" Katherine asked, trying to keep up with the nurse.

"We're still assessing him. At this stage we're trying to determine the damage from a fall. We'll be carrying out a CT shortly.

"Is he conscious?"

"Yes, but not very responsive."

They stopped along the corridor. She pointed to a door. "His daughter is in there. The paramedics said she was having a panic attack when they arrived."

"I'll look after her. Please keep me posted on Mr Walker."

The nurse nodded.

"Thank you."

Katherine stood outside the door for a moment. She took a deep breath. She didn't even know if Anna would want her there. They hadn't parted on any terms except for a lack of trust.

She pushed open the door, unsure what state she would find Anna in. She was sitting on a seat with her back to the door. Katherine could tell she was sobbing from the movements she made.

She didn't want to make her jump, so she spoke softly. "Anna?"

Anna turned and looked at her; she blinked her red, puffy eyes in disbelief. She jumped up and ran to Katherine. Katherine felt herself respond, wrapping her arms tightly around Anna's waist and laying her head against hers.

Anna sobbed; her body vibrated against Katherine's. She pulled away after a few minutes and looked at her.

"How did you know?"

"A blue light and a sixth sense."

Anna looked at her, baffled.

"I saw the ambulance and then couldn't rest until I knew you were both safe. I went to your house, and your neighbour was just locking up. Why didn't you call me?"

Anna shrugged. "I thought we were supposed to be keeping a distance."

"I think your father's medical circumstance negates the need for distance, Anna. Are you all right?"

"I'm fine. Have they said anything about how he is?"

"They are looking at him now, but he's conscious. That's a good sign."

Katherine led her back to where she had been sitting and sat beside her.

"I can't bear the wait. I need to know if he's okay."

"They'll tell us as soon as they know something." Katherine placed her hand on Anna's. "What happened?"

"I'm not sure. I was woken by banging and him yelling. When I got up, he was in a heap at the bottom of the stairs. I think he must have been going to the toilet."

"Did you give him a sleeping tablet?"

"No. We tried them, but he was quite groggy in the mornings, and I struggled to get him up on time to get him ready before I left for work."

Katherine removed her hand from Anna's and stood up. "Anna, I prescribed the tablets to keep Harry safe in bed at night, and you stopped them to suit your schedule."

"Seriously, you're judging me right now?" Anna glared at her. "You abandon us and then dictate the terms of our schedule."

Katherine realised she had opened a can of worms she hadn't intended to. The last thing she wanted was for Anna to ask her to leave. She sat back down. That Anna felt abandoned rocked her to her core. "Sorry, I'm in no position to judge you."

They remained silent until the door opened and the nurse entered.

"Miss Walker, I can take you to see your father now. We've made him comfortable. He is asleep, though, so you can only see him for a few minutes."

Anna nodded.

"How is he doing?" Katherine looked directly at the nurse.

"I'll pop back in a minute and give you a full rundown." She half winked, which Katherine took to mean she wanted to give her the full and frank picture and the basics to Anna so as not to confuse or scare her.

Katherine took herself off to the window and watched the lights of cars moving around the town in the darkness. She instantly regretted it as thoughts of Helena drifted into her mind again. To her relief the nurse soon reappeared.

"The CT has come back clear, but the X-rays show he has sustained a fractured ulna and femoral head. The rest is just a few cuts and bruises. We'll look to operate tomorrow if he's fit enough, he is quite frail. I understand he has Parkinson's."

"Yes, late stage three," Katherine confirmed.

The nurse made a note on her clipboard. "Hopefully it shouldn't cause too many problems but no doubt you are aware of the complications."

Katherine nodded. "Can you take me to him?"

"Sure, it's this way."

She followed the nurse down the corridor and onto a ward.

"He's in the last bay. We'll move him up to geriatric in the morning. Five more minutes."

Katherine nodded and passed her a card. "Thanks for your help. Please call me if there's any change, any time."

Anna was beside Harry, holding his hand. She watched as Anna fumbled in her pocket and brought out a tissue to wipe her eyes. Katherine decided to give her a moment before she approached. Her core ached for the two of them and what was to come.

Harry was going to need so much more care than Anna could give. Even if Katherine could find a way to help them again, it wouldn't be enough. The time had come, and she knew she would have to be the one to push Anna to see it, whether she wanted to or not. After the last few weeks of lies and distrust, she feared there wasn't going to be much to salvage of their relationship, let alone a friendship.

Anna took some persuading to leave the hospital, but she eventually relented, mainly from exhaustion. The car journey home was a silent one; Anna stared out of her window into the darkness. Katherine didn't feel it was time to raise any thoughts of what the future was going to look like; that could wait until the morning.

She pulled on to the drive of Abbey House and turned the engine off. "Come on, I'll walk you home."

Anna didn't respond. Katherine touched her hand, mindful that she may have fallen asleep.

"I don't want to be there alone." Anna turned to look at Katherine. Her eyes puffed red, and strands of her hair stuck to her face.

Katherine reached up and lifted them away. "Do you want to stay here? With me?"

Anna looked through the windscreen and nodded.

Katherine knew it wasn't the best of ideas considering her lawyer's advice for them not to be seen together, but at this point, she didn't really care. Anna needed her, and she was going to be there for her. She led her inside.

"Do you want anything before bed? Tea? Something to

eat? I won't offer you a whisky even though you look like you need one."

Anna attempted a smile, but it didn't form. "No. Thanks. I stink of the hospital."

"Have a shower. You can borrow some clothes. I've got a spare toothbrush somewhere."

Katherine wanted to take her hand and lead her upstairs, but it didn't feel appropriate. Anna followed a few steps behind and took the towel Katherine offered her from the airing cupboard on the landing.

"You know where the shower is; there should be a spare toothbrush in the cabinet."

Katherine sat on the bed in her silk pyjamas and typed out a message to Rebecca whilst she waited for Anna to finish in the shower.

Harry fell and in hospital. Damsel in my shower.

A reply swiftly followed; she knew Rebecca would still be out partying, no doubt drunk.

Is he okay?

He'll live… perhaps not in Nunswick.

Good luck explaining that to the damsel. Don't do anything I wouldn't do.

Hardly appropriate given the circumstances! She needs a friend.

I have nothing else to add here that will be appropriate, I'm drunk and horny.

Then go seek. x

x

Rebecca was one of a kind. Katherine had been out partying with her and then seen her prepare for court the next day, and she had trouble believing they were the same person. She took the term "work hard, play hard" to its fullest extent.

Anna emerged from the bathroom in a pair of Katherine's joggers and a sweatshirt. Her hair was wrapped up in a towel on top of her head.

"Have you got a hairdryer I can borrow?"

"Yes, sit at my dressing table. I'll dry it for you."

Katherine removed the towel from Anna's head and rubbed at her hair. She directed the hairdryer through her long hair, catching glimpses of Anna in the mirror, her forlorn expression unchanged each time. As she blew the last remnants of moisture from the ends of her hair, she thought she saw Anna's lips move in the mirror and turned the hairdryer off.

"Did you say something?"

"No," Anna replied softly.

"Well, all done."

Anna pulled her hair around to her front and stroked it. "Thank you."

"You take my bed. I put clean sheets on this morning."

Anna climbed in. "Where are you going to sleep?"

"I'll grab a blanket and take the sofa. None of the other beds are made up."

"I'm not going to turf you out of your own bed and… I don't want to be alone."

Every part of Katherine wanted to jump into bed with Anna, but this wasn't exactly what she had planned.

"Okay, but keep to your side. And no funny business." Katherine raised her eyebrows at Anna, which finally got a smile out of her.

Katherine climbed in beside her and turned out the

light. She was desperate to reach out to Anna, even if just to hold her. It wasn't as if they were together anymore, but it didn't feel appropriate even as just friends — if that was what they were now.

As she drifted off, she thought about what she would have to do the next day to bring Anna to the realisation that she would no longer be able to care for her father.

CHAPTER 20

*A*nna wrenched her eyes open the next morning. She stretched herself out over the enormous bed, enjoying the softness of the sheets against her face. It was the most comfortable bed she'd ever slept in, and the sheets smelt of lavender washing powder.

It took a moment for her to work out where she was; everything felt different to normal. She sat bolt upright. *Dad.* She jumped out of bed, noticing the other side had been slept in. She desperately tried to recall the last twelve hours. Had she and Katherine? No.

Finding her clothes, she quickly dressed; there was so much to sort before she went back to the hospital. She'd need to book a taxi and call Carrie to say she wouldn't be in today. A sniff of her jumper told her what she needed most was a change of clothes. No doubt Harry would want things taken into the hospital too.

A check of her phone told her it was past nine and Carrie would be wondering where she was. It also told her it was on four percent battery. Katherine really could have woken her.

Anna made her way downstairs to the kitchen where she guessed Katherine would be. She was right. Katherine was sat at the island working away on her laptop.

Anna stood in the doorway for a moment. She felt a little awkward being in Katherine's space now after everything that had been exchanged between them.

Katherine noticed her and greeted her with a friendly smile which instantly put her at ease. "Morning."

"Morning. Thanks for last night."

"You're very welcome."

"We didn't…" Anna trailed off, suddenly regretting asking.

"Really?" Katherine raised her eyebrows. "Do I look like I lure emotional women into my lair and then take advantage of them?"

Anna pulled in her bottom lip. "Possibly not."

Katherine got up. "I would hope if we had, it wouldn't be that unforgettable. Sit, I'll make you some tea."

"I can't. I need to call Carrie, the hospital. I'll need to sort a taxi back there and get some things together for Dad."

"I've called Carrie; she said she doesn't expect to see you for the rest of the week. I've rung the hospital; he's fine. I've cleared my schedule, so I'll be taking you to the hospital, but as for Harry's bits, you'll have to do that."

Anna blinked and sat down at the island. "Thanks."

Katherine eyeballed her cautiously. "Wait. No 'You shouldn't have done that,' or 'You've overstepped'?"

"No, just thanks," Anna replied. She was grateful to

have Katherine back by her side and helping; she'd missed it. They were a team, or at least they had been.

A text message popped up on Anna's phone.

"Have you got a charger?"

"Yes, there's one under the work surface."

Anna looked down, surprised to see an electrical socket on the island.

She read the message as Katherine placed a mug in front of her. It was from Carrie.

Sorry to hear about your dad, we all hope he gets better soon. x

"So, what did the hospital say?" Anna wrapped her hands around the mug.

"He had a good night, and they will operate later today. They said you can see him this morning, although it's not strictly visiting hours."

"Are you sure you're okay to take me?"

"Yes, I only had a meeting today, which has been rescheduled, and a bit of paperwork which I can do later."

"You know what I mean." Anna looked at her but was unable to hold eye contact.

"It's just a ride to the hospital where I'm going to check on my patient. I'll take the risk."

"Thanks again. I do appreciate everything you've done for me. I know it was a risk bringing me here last night, so I really can't thank you enough." Anna gulped the rest of her tea and placed the mug down. "Right, I'll pop home, change, and grabs some things for Dad."

"Do you want me to come with you?"

"Thanks, but I'm sure I'll be fine."

"Your neighbour mentioned some bloodstains; I think

they attempted to clean it. Don't be shocked. It's only a bit of blood."

Anna nodded and gave her half a smile.

Walking back into the house without Harry being there was strange. She wished she'd taken Katherine up on her offer now and had her beside her; everything felt easier with her at her side.

She could see where the neighbour had cleaned some of the blood up; the patch was cleaner than the rest of the carpet. It hit her how different the house was from Katherine's. It was dark, dingy, cluttered, and a little musty.

She hadn't noticed when she had arrived. It was just the old house, but now she realised how much they had let it go. Paint peeled off the walls and cracks had appeared. The carpet was threadbare. It wasn't a place she recognised as home. Her mother would have been devastated to see it.

She wondered if she could use the time off between hospital visits to do it up for him. She felt a little embarrassed to think Katherine had come into her home, which was so in contrast to her own, but she'd never said anything or judged the way they lived.

After a change of clothes, she rummaged under her bed and found a small bag that would do for her dad's things. She took it through to his room and pulled back the curtains. She was faced with the same dismal scene. So much needed doing.

With a few items stored in the bag, Anna made her way back to Katherine's. She didn't know how she would be coping now if it wasn't for her. The immense relief she felt when Katherine had appeared at the hospital was overwhelming. She was still angry at her, but in that moment as she dried her hair for her, she had felt the need to say out loud how she felt. "I love you," she had whispered, not ready for Katherine to hear it.

She wasn't sure at this stage if the fundamentals of their relationship could even be fixed. Any talk of love at this stage would only complicate matters and put pressure where it wasn't needed. There was trust to rebuild after Katherine had lied about why she broke things off with her, regardless of why she had done it.

During the car journey to the hospital, Anna made plans for how she would fix the house up, where she would start. His bedroom was probably best as he would need to use it a lot. Katherine had been quiet the whole journey, as they approached the ward he had been moved to, she stopped suddenly.

"Be prepared, his bruises will have come out. He may look a little worse than you remember from last night."

Anna nodded, and they entered the ward.

Katherine was right: Her dad looked like he'd picked a fight with a lion and lost. His face was bruised and scratched up, and an arm was in plaster.

"Don't mind me if I don't get up," Harry said with a smile.

"Don't be silly, Dad."

"Good to see you, doc." Harry gave Katherine a wink.

"Harry." Katherine nodded at him.

A nurse entered with an iPad. "Ah, good, you're here. I was about to run him through everything. Take a seat."

Anna took the only seat by the bed and watched Katherine as she walked around to the window.

"We'll be doing a hip replacement today, Harry, because you have a fracture in your femoral neck. That's the bit that connects the top of your leg with the ball joint of the hip." She made a rather hash job with her hands to try and demonstrate, but Harry nodded his understanding.

"Now you'll be needing a general anaesthetic. The anaesthetist will be down shortly to go through that with you as it can be a little more complicated in Parkinson's patients."

"Why more complicated?" Anna didn't like the sound of where this was going. She looked to Katherine, who stepped forward to reassure her.

"It's more about the side effects after than the surgery itself. When the brain is in a fragile state like Harry's, then it can get a little agitated from the anaesthetic."

"Yes exactly," the nurse confirmed. "Following the surgery, you may want to wait twenty-four hours before coming in again. Let him settle."

"That's a good idea, Anna." Katherine nodded at her.

"Now, Harry, following the surgery, your sensitivity to the medication you are on may increase or decrease, so you let us know if you are experiencing any symptoms you don't think you should be. We'll come and get you at midday; it should take a couple of hours." The nurse turned to Anna. "We'll ring you of course once we're done and let you know how he is. Then, if all is well, you can come back tomorrow evening during visiting hours or possibly even the next day. He should be back on this ward by then."

Katherine left with the nurse, leaving Anna alone to fuss over her dad.

"I'm sorry, Dad. This is all my fault. I should have got up to help you or fitted a stair gate."

He clasped her hand the best he could with his good arm. "There, there, it was just an accident. I lost my footing, that's all. Could have happened to anyone."

"But it didn't, Dad, and now look at you." Anna looked at all the machines he was plugged into. "You just get better and get back home with me, all right?"

He nodded. "Sure thing, love. I see the doc is back by your side?"

Anna pursed her lips. "Don't read anything into it, Dad. She just gave me a lift, nothing more."

A different nurse came and took some readings from the machines.

"How are you feeling, Harry?"

"All right. A bit tired."

The nurse shot a look at Anna. "You were very restless in the night."

"It's more noise than I'm used to, people coming and going and prodding all night."

The nurse smiled at him.

"I'll go, Dad, and let you have a rest before you go down to the operating theatre. I'll see you tomorrow maybe."

"All right, love."

She kissed Harry on the head and squeezed his hand, trying hard not to think of him lying helpless on a metal table in a few short hours. "Don't you boss the nurses about."

Harry chuckled, and Anna backed away, hoping it wouldn't be the last time she saw him.

She found Katherine in the corridor reading a notice board.

"That was quick."

"He was tired."

Katherine nodded. "Let's get you home. You look tired out too."

Anna stared out the window of the car as they drove. Hospitals were tiring places; she felt exhausted and was dying for another shower.

"Is he going to be okay?" she asked, continuing to stare out of the window.

"Of course. It's a very routine procedure these days, but with any surgery there are risks. Don't worry, they know what they are doing."

"How long until he's out of hospital do you think?"

"Perhaps a week, all being well. Maybe two."

"That gives me enough time to make a good start on sorting the house."

"Sorting the house?" Katherine asked.

"Yes, you've seen it; it's in a bit of a state. I'll have to get the council to come and install a stairlift for him."

"Anna, are you still…" Katherine shook her head and twisted her lips.

"What?"

"He needs a care home, Anna! Why do you refuse to see it?"

"I can't just leave him to fester in a care home."

"You'll happily let him fester at your home."

Anna turned her head to look at Katherine. "Excuse me?"

"It's not healthy him being trapped in that house. Open the door and let him out before you suffocate him."

Anna couldn't believe the words that had just left Katherine's mouth. Even if someone thought that, it really shouldn't be spoken.

"I'm sorry, I shouldn't have said that, but stop letting one bad incident dictate everything. Your mum died, it was horrible, but don't you think you're projecting that experience onto the care home? It was where she died, not the reason she died. I didn't stop driving a car because my wife and child were crushed to death in one. What would be so bad about letting your dad have some company, a laugh with some new friends, professional care?"

Anna didn't want to answer that; she could sense the scary Dr Katherine emerging, the one that could make you feel small and pathetic. She'd never seen Katherine lose it before, but she was beginning to think she might be witnessing it.

Katherine laughed, and Anna shot her a look.

"You're frightened, aren't you? That once he's in a home you'll have nothing and no one will need you. You'll have left your life in London behind for nothing. So what if you lose his house? You'll find somewhere to live, and as for the memories of your mother, they're not in the house. Voices don't live in walls; they live in here." Katherine tapped the side of her head. When Anna said nothing, she seemed to grow disgusted by her passenger. "Christ. I never pegged you as selfish, Anna."

Anna gawped and was about to muster a response when Katherine fired up again.

"You are barely keeping yourself together. How on earth are you going to nurse someone? Nursing and caring are very different things, Anna. Sometimes our best can never be enough; that's why we must understand our limitations and let go of the things we can't control. There are people out there whose best is good enough because they've undertaken extensive training. It's time to let them do their job."

"I'm fine," Anna slipped in lamely as soon as Katherine drew a breath.

"What about your panic attack on the way to the hospital? The paramedic needed to be focused on your dad, but there you were breathing into a paper bag."

Anna made a mental note that the next-door neighbour was a gossip.

"Take last night as a warning and be brave. Let him go."

Silence and tension filled the car until Katherine pulled up on the drive of Abbey House, the familiar gravel sound crunching under the tyres.

"I'm glad to know your true feelings, Katherine. I think I'll go it alone from now on." Anna unclipped her seat belt. "I'll get a taxi to the hospital in future, but thank you for being there the last few days. I wouldn't want to compromise your career further."

Katherine wrung her hands on the steering wheel of her parked car. "That's a bit dramatic, don't you think, just because we disagree?"

Anna decided to speak plainly; after all, Katherine had

done so. "I don't think it's dramatic at all. If you're not with me, you're against me. I don't need that kind of negativity. I don't need another dishonest doctor in my life."

Katherine glared at her. "You know why I lied."

Anna climbed out of the car and leaned back in. "It doesn't stop me from being angry and disappointed. If you had just spoken to me instead of trying to control everything *yourself*, because you think you know what is best, it wouldn't have come to this. I thought doctors were supposed to listen. What hurts the most is you were willing to give us up without a fight. I know you think it was admirable, but really it was just shitty."

She slammed the door shut as she exited the car, glad to have had the last word.

CHAPTER 21

Katherine popped a couple of paracetamol in her mouth and washed them down with a glass of water. It was never advisable to drink to forget, but last night it had been her only option. She'd had to stop herself from ringing Anna twice and once from going over to her house to apologise.

She eventually settled it with herself, over far too much whisky, that although she didn't feel great about what she had said, it had needed saying and Anna was best left to deal with it. At least she had no surgery that day, although she could have used the distraction.

She regretted making the pact with Rebecca about how many hours she should work, but Rebecca had said it was in place for moments such as these when she was tempted to use work as a distraction from her problems. Technically it was only paid work she had promised not to take on, and Katherine had had an idea that might circumvent the pact.

A trip to the tearoom was in order, as was one of

Gloria's vitamin drinks. The cabinet was just being restocked as Katherine entered; it was overflowing with inviting cakes. She always got the munchies with hangovers and looked away to resist temptation.

"Anna's back on the coffee; seems your effect on her has worn off."

On any normal day Katherine might have given Gloria a piece of her mind, but today she needed to extract some information from her, so settled for a smile instead.

"Vitamin juice for you, or have you moved on to the strong stuff too?" Gloria continued.

Katherine frowned. "Juice, please."

"Have you heard about Harry?"

"Yes, I've been — " Katherine stopped herself before she could reveal too much; she knew she had to be more careful until she could establish who had reported her to the GMC. It had to be someone in the village, and although it seemed as if Gloria and Anna had a bond, Katherine didn't trust her. "Yes, I did. Poor man."

"More to add to that poor girl's woes."

Gloria disappeared into the kitchen. Katherine took the opportunity to have a nose around. She spotted what she was hoping to find, a notice board. Pinned to it was one of Gloria's amusing business cards, a removals business card, someone advertising their services as a cleaner and someone looking for a cleaner.

"Looking to advertise, doctor?" Gloria asked, having suddenly reappeared.

Katherine jumped. "No. What do people do around here for entertainment or exercise?"

Gloria pouted and rubbed her chin.

"They go to the pub, I suppose."

Katherine was about to ask about the exercise aspect and realised Gloria most likely meant the walk to the pub covered that element.

"Are there no groups in the village?"

"Groups?" Gloria tilted her head.

"Walking groups, that sort of thing," Katherine suggested.

"There used to be, but the woman running it moved away and it stopped."

"What about fitness groups?"

"Well, there's nowhere to hold things like that, is there?"

Gloria sounded as if Katherine should know that, so she decided to answer the question with a question. "Is there not?"

"No, the village hall burnt down, didn't it? They built a playground on it rather than rebuilding it."

Katherine sucked on her straw as Gloria proceeded to fill her in on the shortcomings of the parish council and local council.

The phone rang out through her handbag and gave her the chance to escape the tearoom now that she had harvested the information she needed. She answered the call from Rebecca as soon as she stepped out onto the high street and the tearoom door was firmly shut behind her.

"Hey, how's Harry doing?"

"Fine, I think. He had his operation yesterday."

"Poor chap. How's the damsel?"

Katherine rolled her eyes and began the walk home. "Unlikely to speak to me ever again."

"Oh dear, what have you done now?"

"I kind of let rip." Katherine winced as she recalled the previous day. "She's still in complete denial about a care home for Harry. I had hoped his fall would have at least brought her around to the idea."

"It's an inevitability. Perhaps she wants to be the one to choose when it happens," Rebecca said.

"No, that would make sense if it were the case. She just can't accept that it must happen. I guess deep down she knows if Harry goes to a care home, he'll die there, which he will, and she doesn't want to be the one that put him there. Her mother died in a care home, and I think it still haunts her. You'd be proud, though. I even used the analogy of me driving a car despite losing Helena in one to try and convince her she was making the wrong decision."

"Wow, we have come on."

"I actually feel I have, Becks. I don't know if it was letting myself fall for Anna that did it or just my new life here. I have so many ideas of things I want to do. Non-stressful things, before you lecture me. I can finally see a future."

"And does that future include a certain tour guide?"

"Let's say that's unlikely. I said some awful things, Becks. I basically told her she was suffocating him." Katherine closed her eyes at the memory of her behaviour.

"Shit, you're a bad friend."

"Sometimes it takes a good friend to tell you the truth."

Rebecca laughed. "Yeah, I know that one all right. If you've left the damsel to deal with her own distress, don't you think when it all goes horribly wrong she'll resent you for not being there for her? Or is your devious plan to rush in at the eleventh hour and save her?"

"GMC problem aside, she said she wants to deal with everything on her own now. I'm sure she'll come to realise she can't cope, and she needs to be alone when she realises it."

Rebecca tutted. "You've thrown her to the wolves, and now you're going to sit back with the popcorn and watch."

"It's the only way. I thought she was at a breaking point before Harry's fall, but she seems more determined to manage now, like she has something to prove. I know she's a bit messed up with what happened to her mother; she's trying to avoid a repeat of it, but history repeats itself. We just have to learn to accept it."

"Well, it sounds like it's all happening in Nunswick," Rebecca said sarcastically. "How about I come down at the weekend? I could use some entertainment."

"Sounds like a plan. I'll restock the cellar!"

"What are you up to today?"

"Did you know there is literally nothing for people to do in this village? No activities, groups, anything?"

"Oh lordy."

"What?"

"Project Damsel is off, and so you're on to something else."

"I just think there should be opportunities in the village for people to meet and share interests, even get fit. They don't even have anywhere to meet. The village hall burned down in the nineties and wasn't replaced. The parish council meet at the church, which I might add doesn't have a hall; they just sit in the choir stalls. This village is dead, Becks, full of walking zombies. The over-sixties only venture out at night to the pub, the over-eighties never seem to leave their homes, but then, why would they when there is nothing to do? Something needs to be done."

"Don't tell me you're going to build them a village hall?"

"Don't be ridiculous. Even you know I couldn't afford that. Anna did mention that the abbey are expanding their visitor centre. I wonder if they might have room for activities."

"Sounds like a good place to start. Better go; I have an arraignment hearing about to start."

"A new case?" Katherine asked as she approached her driveway.

"Yep, and it's a biggy."

"See you soon then." Katherine hung up and, instead of making her way up the drive, walked into the abbey car park.

CHAPTER 22

*A*nna paced the car park of Baycroft Care Home. She'd taken a taxi, and her dad had been due to arrive in the hospital transfer ambulance ten minutes ago. She'd looked the care home up online. It seemed okay and had specialist Parkinson's care. Not that it mattered all that much; as soon as social services bucked their ideas up and assessed the house for his return, she'd be over to collect him.

It was a thirty-minute drive from Nunswick and had cost a fair whack for the taxi. She had contemplated asking Katherine to bring her, but after their last conversation, when she had said she would go it alone in future, Anna realised she had put a final nail in the idea of anything between them.

Katherine had spoken her mind, more fervently than ever before, about Harry's situation. Anna knew if she had involved her again, she would be sitting in her rather lovely car getting another earbashing about how he should be staying in the home. She couldn't go back on it now, even though she missed the annoying, beautiful doctor even more than she had realised she would.

Anna analysed the care home; it was a newish building and didn't look as dreary as the one her mum had been in. It had a large car park at the front, was nicely landscaped, and appeared meticulously maintained. Noticing it was two-storey, she hoped her dad would have a room on the ground floor so he wouldn't be tempted to take the stairs.

She shivered and regretted not bringing a cardigan; the front of the home was north-facing, so at least the garden looked to be south-facing. Not that her dad was one for sitting out in the garden; he was much happier in front of the television or reading a book.

The sound of an engine diverted her attention to the road. An ambulance drove past and turned up the driveway, pulling up in front of the building. Relief swept over her at her dad's beaming face looking through the window.

The driver wheeled him out of the back of the ambulance; he rested his plastered arm on the hospital bag on his lap.

"How are you doing, Dad?" Anna leaned down and gave him a kiss.

"Oh, I'm all right. This is all a bit of a fuss. I told them I could take a taxi."

The driver shook his head. "I keep telling him it's all part of the service."

"Well, it's very kind of you to lug an old man around," Harry replied loudly over his shoulder.

The driver pushed him through to a spacious reception

area. Anna followed with a small suitcase of belongings she'd brought from home.

A woman a little younger than Anna met them and introduced herself as Lucy.

"I'll be taking care of you, Mr Walker, and when I'm not here, it will be Susan; she's my counterpart. If you need anything, just let us know."

Harry nodded.

"Your room is on the ground floor. We know you're a little unsteady on your feet, so it's best to keep you down here."

Lucy must have noticed the relief on Anna's face as she gave her a reassuring smile.

"Shall I give you a tour of downstairs and then show you to your room so you can get settled?"

Anna looked at Harry. "That sound okay, Dad?"

"Oh, yes, lead on."

Anna relieved the ambulance driver and took up position behind Harry. Lucy led the way out of the reception area into a large, two-storey glass atrium that overlooked the garden and surrounding countryside. Even Anna's jaw dropped; it was stunning. It was a lot bigger than the front aspect of the building suggested.

"This is the main area, where meals are served if residents would prefer to eat outside their rooms. We fully assist them if they require it. It leads out onto a lovely patio area which we use in good weather. Over there is our library." Lucy pointed to a door at the far end of the atrium. "We work within the local authority library system to borrow any books we don't have; you only have to ask. There is a craft and hobby studio next door to that and a games room and a quiet lounge. We also have a movie club, Harry."

Harry's ears pricked up, and he grinned. "Movie club?"

"It's open to everyone, but it does seem to be dominated by the chaps now. It might be something you'd like to go along to. It's on three times a week, and you can suggest movies you'd like to see and vote on them. We have a big screen in the games room. It's more of a social event really, to get like-minded residents together."

Harry's face lit up. "Sounds great. Do you have popcorn?"

Lucy smiled at him. "We certainly do."

"You're only here for a few days, remember, Dad," Anna said.

Harry nodded.

"It's very nice," Anna added, not wanting to sound negative.

Lucy smiled and continued. "There's a small shop if they need anything. We can get anything in for them if they have special requirements. Let me show you to your room now, Harry; it's along here."

She led them back out of the atrium and around a glass-walled corridor that surrounded it. Lucy stopped at a door not far down the corridor.

"And here's you." Lucy held the door open as Anna wheeled her dad through.

It was larger than Anna had expected, with a big window to the front. A single bed was central to the room along with a set of drawers and a wardrobe. A sitting area was set out by the window, including a television, chair, and table.

"All our rooms come with their own en-suite." Lucy gestured with her hand to the door in the corner of the room. "Shall we get you out of there and into your chair, Harry?"

Harry nodded his agreement, and Anna left Lucy to deal with Harry. She wasn't sure of his capabilities or strength since his hip operation. He shuffled slowly to his chair, assisted by Lucy, and sat down.

He shuffled about a bit to get comfortable. "It's not like my chair at home, but I'm sure it will do."

"I'll leave you to it for a bit, let you unpack and find your way around. If you need anything, just press the buzzer." Lucy pointed to a white box with a red button beside the bed. She approached Harry. "It's lunch soon; perhaps we can introduce you to some of the other residents."

"All right, love," Harry replied, eyes glued to the television even though it wasn't on.

It didn't go unnoticed by Anna that Harry's usual response was now directed at someone else rather than her. There was a pang of relief mixed with guilt in her stomach.

Lucy smiled and left.

"Pass me the remote, will you, love?" Harry gesticulated at the table in front of him as soon as the door closed.

Anna passed it to him with a grin, glad to see that after the last week of emotion, at least he was the same old Harry.

"Anna, it's got Sky Television!"

"I doubt it, Dad."

"This is a Sky remote, look." Harry held it up, grinning from ear to ear.

She was pleased to see him so happy but felt the disappointment that would come once he returned home. She began to unpack his clothes into a chest of drawers and inspected the en-suite. A large glass panel ran down one side with a seat and a shower head above. It was much nicer than their pokey bathroom at home.

She placed his toothbrush and toothpaste on the shelf in front of a large mirror, catching sight of herself in it. She rarely had time to look in the mirror beyond removing a few unwanted white eyebrow hairs. The large mirror reflected an image she barely recognised. She looked tired, more worn around the edges than ever before; she certainly wasn't the same Anna from even six months ago.

She'd always paid so much attention to her appearance when she was in the city. Although as a researcher she would dress smart-casual, she'd always taken the time to keep her appearance in check. She counted herself lucky now if she had time to brush her hair before leaving the house in her usual green Abbey jumper and light brown chinos. It was hardly the look she had envisaged for herself in her late thirties.

At least it was all for a good cause; if her dad was happy that was what mattered, and he needed all the love and care she could give him whilst he was still with her. She breathed deeply, trying to calm her thoughts about all the things that would need doing to get the house sorted. She'd spent the last few days clearing out unwanted clutter and cleaning, trying to make the place feel a bit fresher before the social services visit. All it had told her was how much more work needed doing than she had realised.

Some of the window frames were rotten. Although they were the council's problem, to deal with it would still cause disruption, and she'd have to be the one to hound them to get it done. She'd taken down all the curtains and net curtains in the house and soaked them in the garden. She had vowed not to return the net curtains, but she remembered her mum making them and couldn't bring herself to throw them away, so back up they went.

She was grateful that the garden was small and easily maintainable. It took a quick mow and a few weeds to be teased from the patio for it to look reasonably tidy, not that she was sure they would even look outside.

Even a hoovering of the carpets had led to a realisation that they would have to go. That would be their cost to bear, or more likely hers; she didn't feel she could ask her dad for money. She had some money put aside for a rainy day, though she had hoped she could use it for a holiday that summer. That was before everything had changed. She hadn't even thought about a holiday since moving home. The best she could hope for was a sit-down whilst she drank a coffee she knew she shouldn't be drinking.

There was a knock at the door and the sound of it opening. Anna walked back into the bedroom to see Lucy placing some towels on the bed.

"I presume you'll need towels, Harry, as you've come straight from the hospital. You can bring your own from home if you like, but you're welcome to use ours."

"Thanks," Anna replied. Her dad was too engrossed in the television to have heard. "He's just discovered you have Sky Television, so good luck moving him from his chair. Ever."

Lucy grinned. "Oh, that reminds me." She knelt beside Harry and took the remote. "It's voice-activated. What films do you like, Harry?"

"War films."

She held a button on the side. "War films," she said, a list of war films popped up on the screen.

Harry's eyebrows shot up; he looked at Anna in disbelief.

Lucy placed the remote in his hand and guided his thumb to the button on the side.

"Pick one."

She pressed his thumb into it.

Harry scanned the screen. "*The Great Escape.*"

The Great Escape started playing.

"Will you look at that," Harry said in amazement. "The wonders of modern technology."

Lucy stood and joined Anna. "It's much easier for our residents, especially those that struggle with motor functions. I'll be back in a few minutes to take you to lunch, Harry."

"I better go, Dad. I've got a taxi booked to take me home. Social services are due soon to check the house over. We'll have you home as soon as we can, just need to get a few modifications done. I'm hoping we can get you a stair-lift fitted."

"All right, love."

"I'll come back tomorrow and see how you're settling in." She kissed him on the head.

She hated leaving him there, all alone. What if he didn't like the food or couldn't get to the toilet in time? She hesitated as she left the room, making her way slowly to the door. Harry was too engrossed in the television to even notice she was leaving.

Lucy was just coming down the corridor.

"Lucy, what is for lunch?"

She thought for a moment. "It's roast chicken or lasagne today. Does he like either?"

Anna took a deep breath. "His favourites."

"Perfect." Lucy placed a reassuring hand on Anna's arm. "Don't worry, we'll look after him."

Anna walked back to the reception area feeling surplus to requirements suddenly. She waited for the taxi outside, pleased to feel it had warmed up a bit. Her thoughts began to wander without a focus, so she withdrew her phone and wrote a list of jobs that still needed to be done before the council visit.

CHAPTER 23

*A*nna wiped the sweat from her brow. The council were due shortly, and she still had a few last-minute tasks to do to make sure the house looked perfect — well, as perfect as it could be without a full renovation.

A knock at the door told her it was too late. She smoothed her shirt down and opened the door. On the other side stood a rather aggressive-looking woman who reminded her of a brutal music teacher from school. She came complete with a clipboard, biro, and glasses with string around them.

"I'm from social services, come to do your home assessment for a Harry Walker." She flashed a card on a lanyard at Anna but didn't give her time to read it.

"Come in, I'm his daughter, Anna." Anna held the door open wide for her.

The woman entered and immediately started scribbling notes on her clipboard with ruthless efficiency as she examined the sitting room.

"Do you live here too?" She didn't even take her eyes off her clipboard.

"Yes."

"You'll be his carer?" She spoke as quickly as she scribbled.

"Yes."

"We'll need to see a care plan for him."

"A care plan?"

The woman finally looked up and glared at Anna. "Yes, so we can see how you are going to manage his needs and who is going to support you."

"O... kay," Anna replied, unsure what that would entail.

The woman poked her head into the kitchen and then turned to her with a look of disbelief. "Can I ask if you work, Miss Walker?"

"Yes."

"Full time?"

Anna nodded.

"How do you suppose to be a full-time carer when you work full time? This isn't even going to be a full-time job; it's twenty-four seven, three hundred sixty-five days a year. You are aware that your father's condition will continue to deteriorate, often quite rapidly towards the end."

The woman paused and waited for a response from Anna. With none forthcoming, she began again.

"We can make the adaptations, but I strongly believe you are putting off the inevitable and at great risk, Miss Walker. I would recommend putting your father's needs first."

"What do you mean?" Anna pulled herself upright.

"In these situations, we find that family keep the patient at home to ease their own conscience. Often resulting in some form of neglect which lands them back in hospital."

Anna felt like slapping the woman for her frankness. The woman must have sensed it.

"Not that I'm insinuating any of that would happen here, Miss Walker. I'm talking generally."

The woman sounded just like Katherine.

"You don't know a Dr Atkinson, do you?"

The woman shook her head. "Should I?"

"Never mind."

She handed Anna a card. "I'll give you time to think about it. Ring that number if you want to go ahead. It's usually a two-week wait."

Anna's jaw dropped. "He had to go into temporary accommodation at a care home this morning because it has taken you until now to come out and assess the house. Now he'll have to stay there for another two weeks!"

"Maybe more."

Anna collapsed on the sofa after the woman had left. She felt drained; the woman had come in and sucked the life and optimism out of her. At least she had a clearer idea in her head of the way forward; sacrifices would have to be made, and she'd have to speak to Carrie.

Anna waited for Carrie to finish up her tour, a tour that should have been done by herself, before approaching her.

"Hey, we didn't expect to see you here. How's your dad?"

"He'll survive to watch another war film, don't you worry."

"Good. What brings you here?"

"I'm going to have to be Dad's carer full time from now on. I'm going to have to hand my notice in."

Carrie raised her eyebrows. "Seriously? But you love your job. I can't pretend I'm not gutted, but we'll support you, whatever you choose, even though you're the best tour guide we have. I won't take your notice yet, though. Give it a few days. Let things settle."

Anna nodded her agreement even though she knew nothing would change.

"When is he coming out of the hospital?"

"He was moved into temporary accommodation this morning over at Baycroft."

Carrie nodded. "Oh yeah, my aunt was in there. Nice place."

"They wouldn't let him home until social services assessed the house, which they only bothered to do earlier today. Now he'll be stuck in there another two weeks."

"Won't they let him stay at Baycroft?"

"I don't know. He's coming home anyway."

Carrie frowned.

Anna could feel her blood pressure rising. "Don't you start as well, Carrie. I've had Katherine badgering me since we met to pack him off to a care home. Even the bloody social services woman thought I was mad."

"Seems everyone is on the same hymn sheet except

you. Have you even spoken to your dad, asked him what he wants?"

"No. Katherine said I should."

"Well, I say the same." Carrie folded her arms over her chest, though her tone was gentle. "Talk it over with him. Surely it should be his decision where he wants to be. As I said, Baycroft is wonderful. It was only built a few years ago; it's got all the mod cons."

Anna couldn't disagree; from what she'd seen that morning it looked like a decent place, but it wasn't somewhere they could afford for him to stay.

CHAPTER 24

*A*nna felt a little apprehensive entering the care home the next day. Having slept poorly, she had been in a bad mood since she'd dragged herself out of bed. So much needed doing that it was starting to weigh on her. She'd spent most of the night juggling it around in her mind, trying to order the jobs by importance.

She was met with smiles as she signed in at reception and forced herself to engage with the staff if only to try and snap herself out of her mood. It seemed to help, and she entered her dad's room with a fresh smile on her face. She was determined not to let him know she wasn't having the best day.

"Hey, Dad, how are you?"

"All right, love. A bit stiff in the hip, but they have me doing physio, gentle stuff, you know."

"Good, you'll soon have your dancing shoes back on."

Harry laughed.

"Did you sleep all right?" Anna grabbed the spare chair from the corner of the room and placed it beside him.

"Yep, and before you ask, the food is great too. What did the woman from the council have to say?"

"They can make all the changes we need, but it will be at least two weeks. Do you think you can cope here that long?"

Harry took a moment to respond, looking at her directly when he did. "You know I'm not going to get any better, don't you, love? I'm going to get a lot worse, and I can't ask you to keep on looking after me."

Anna felt breathless. "I don't mind, Dad, honestly. Mum would have wanted you at home with me."

"Anna, your mum's not here, but I am, and I'm telling you I don't want you to do this. It's your decision. If you want me home, I'll come, but I'm telling you I'd rather be here."

Anna opened her mouth to speak, but Harry pre-empted her.

"No, I'm not just saying that. You've looked after me so well these past months, and I'm grateful to you, more than I can tell you, kid, but I really do like it here. I've even met up with a chum from my old work. He's been here for five years. There's always someone to chat to and people my age. We talk about old times; we even have the same lingo you youngsters don't understand. I can get up when I want and not when you need me to."

"But I'd give up work, Dad. I'd be with you all the time. We'd be working to your schedule, not mine. I'm not giving up; I can do this."

He stared at her with his kind, warm eyes. "No, you're not giving up, Anna. I know you'll never give up trying your best, but I'm asking you, for me, to channel your best somewhere else now, into your life, not mine. I will die here, but that won't be your fault. It won't be anyone's fault; it's just life. Now go away, make a life for yourself, but promise to pop back occasionally and tell me how fantastic it is, all right? If you've got any sense at all, you'll make sure the doc is part of it."

Anna wiped away the tears that were resting in her eyes. She suddenly felt a great sense of relief — that she had done all she could, and it had been enough, but it was now at an end.

"You know we'd have to give the house up."

"I wondered as much. Would they not let you stay in it?"

"I've only been there a few months, and my name isn't on the tenancy or any of the bills. I've got no rights. Plus, it wouldn't be the same there without you."

Harry put his hands together and looked down at them shaking. Anna wasn't sure if he was sad because she'd be homeless and they would lose their family home or because she might ask him to come home.

"Look, Dad, I'm sure I can find somewhere else, a new start for both of us?" She placed her hands on his, and he looked up with a smile. "After all, our memories are in here." She tapped his head.

Harry's face lit up. "Really?"

"If it's what you want."

"Good, 'cos I've already told them they're stuck with me."

Anna deflated. "You can't stay here, Dad. We couldn't afford it. I thought you meant we'd find you another home."

Harry shook his head. "No, no, listen. A lady came down from the office this morning and spoke to me about it. She said because of my Parkinson's the NHS will pay for some of it; the council will pay some, too, and the rest I can cover from my pension. I don't get left much, but it's enough for a few things from the shop if I need them. I don't need much else, do I, love?"

"Let me check the details with them before you get too excited."

He barrelled on. "I'm serious about the doctor too. Perhaps you can stop in with her; it must be lonely for her in that big house. Now she's not my doctor, there's no reason you can't be together."

"What do you mean she's not your doctor anymore?" Anna asked, sure she couldn't have heard correctly.

"A new doc came to visit me this morning, says he's taking over. He was ever such a nice chap. His dad had Parkinson's too."

"What? She's taken you off her patient list, and without talking to me first." Anna could feel her lip curling into a snarl but stopped it. "She's unbelievable." Anna paused and thought for a moment. "Hang on, what did you mean there's no reason why we can't be together now?"

"I read that letter from the doctor council people. I assume she broke it off with you because she couldn't be my doctor and your girlfriend at the same time."

Anna nodded. "It's about right, Dad. But she still lied to me about why she broke up, and she lied to the council, too, and asked me to lie too."

"We all make mistakes and quite often in the name of

love. Don't you see? She didn't choose to stay my doctor for me; she did it for you."

"Well, if she's taken you off her books, then it's clear she doesn't want anything more to do with either of us." Anna tried not to choke over the words as her throat tightened. The thought that Katherine might have had enough of her and her dramatic life squeezed the air out of her.

"Maybe it means she wants everything to do with us."

"I doubt it, Dad. She would have spoken to me first."

"Well, I'm sure you'll sort it out between you. Now I've got places to be, people to see. One of the chaps wants me to play cards with him."

"Dad, you can't hold cards."

"That's the game: this chap has Parkinson's, too, and the others bet on who they think can hold their pack the longest."

Anna couldn't help but laugh. "That's ridiculous."

"It's great fun. The best bit is I don't have to pick them up; the other chaps do that. Now get yourself back to work and go and do something you enjoy for once. I'll be fine here."

"All right, Dad. I'm going to check with the manager that you can stay here before I leave."

She kissed him on the head.

"Bye, love."

The lady at reception confirmed what Harry had said, and Anna walked out of the home feeling a little lighter. Yet the niggle in her gut told her not everything was fully resolved.

As the taxi pulled up outside the cottage, she realised

she was going to need a cheap run-around. She'd had a driver's license since she was eighteen but gave up her car when she went to the city. When she got together with Jessica, she'd driven her car but hadn't had the need for one of her own. Now there was a need. If she was going to get to see her dad a couple of times a week, it would be crazy to keep paying for taxis. With house repairs no longer needed, she mentally reclassified the carpet fund as a car fund.

She rang Carrie as soon she stepped out of the taxi, hoping she would still have a job.

"Hi, Anna, how's things?"

"My dad has decided he's staying at the care home. Have I still got a job?"

"Of course you have." Carrie chuckled as she spoke.

Anna let out a sigh of relief. She had nowhere to live, but she could at least feed herself.

"So he was taken in by Baycroft then? I told you it was a great place."

"It seems you were right," Anna replied, twisting her lips.

"Well, I'll expect to see you Monday then."

"Thanks, Carrie. I appreciate it. Sorry for messing you around."

"Not a problem. I'm just glad I don't have to do any more tours; they really are exhausting. I can't understand how you've managed."

Anna laughed as she extracted her key from the front door. "I'm beginning to wonder myself."

She hung up and collapsed onto the sofa. She felt free but as empty as her dad's chair beside her. Katherine had been right: it was nice to feel needed. Yet it had only been a few months and she'd already lost her grounding, her identity. She had been a girlfriend and a carer; now she was neither of them. She was just Anna, and just Anna didn't have a clue what to do with herself.

She tried to think back to who she'd been before she returned to Nunswick, what she'd be doing, where she'd be going, and with whom. She needed to move on, and to do that she knew she would have to get answers from Katherine as to why she had taken her dad off her books. Whatever the reason she had for doing it, Katherine could have at least had the decency to warn her first. Anna's stomach knotted up with anger; it would need doing now.

CHAPTER 25

*R*ebecca baked her legs on a sun lounger as Katherine stepped out onto the patio with a jug of Pimm's and two glasses.

Rebecca grinned. "Ah, what a pleasant sight."

"Me or the Pimm's?" Katherine questioned.

"The Pimm's of course."

Katherine pretended to look hurt and poured her a glass.

Rebecca eyed it. "I've worked late every night this week; not a drop of alcohol has touched my lips. Have you heard anything from Adrian or the GMC since we last spoke?"

Katherine passed Rebecca a glass. "Well, a lot has changed, even since this morning."

"Do tell." Rebecca gulped at her Pimm's and gesticulated at Katherine for a top-up.

"I emailed Adrian this morning, asking him to pass an updated response to the GMC. I've admitted everything, and I'll take my punishment."

Rebecca dropped her sunglasses down her nose and shifted on her sun lounger. "Seriously?"

"It's what I should have done in the first place; Anna was right. I am a dishonest doctor, and it doesn't sit right with me."

"You did it for the right reason."

"Is there such a thing as being dishonest for the right reason? If I ever want a future with her, it must be with a clean slate. I couldn't walk around the village with her, having denied it to the council. People would never stop gossiping. You know it shows everything about the case online and will likely be leaked to the local papers at some point."

"I'm confused. Surely if you get suspended you can't be his doctor anymore."

Katherine took a seat on the sun lounger beside Rebecca. "I'm not his doctor. His care home is out of our district; in fact, it's over the county border, so it belongs to a completely different council altogether. He already has a new doctor, Dr Wilson. I contacted him as soon as the transfer request came into the surgery yesterday, and he's already been in to see him."

Rebecca squinted and shook her head. "But I thought the care home is just temporary?"

"It was as far as I knew. The last time I saw Anna, her intentions seemed to be sorting the house out for Harry's return."

"Shit... I wonder how Anna took all that. Won't she be pissed that you're not his doctor anymore?"

"I'm sure I'll find out soon enough, and the glory of it

is that it won't be my fault. Finally she can't be mad at me for something."

"It also means you're free to date." Rebecca winked at Katherine and put her sunglasses back on.

"It's a stretch that she'll ever speak to me again, let alone date me." Katherine stretched back on the lounger and poked at the fruit in her glass with a straw. "But one can hope, and at least with the council off my back, there will be nothing in my way at least."

"She loves you; that has to count for something, even if she hates you."

"Wait, what?" Katherine sat bolt upright.

Rebecca nodded. "She told me the Sunday we had lunch."

Katherine's mouth fell open. "You didn't think to tell me that before now?"

"Oh no. I thought about it, but it wasn't up to me to tell you. If she had been ready to tell you, you would know." Rebecca raised her eyebrows at Katherine; she stuck out her tongue in return.

They had been in a very different place then. Katherine was under no pretence that Anna would still feel that way after everything that had happened. It was gutting to think that Anna had at some point fallen in love with her; she had felt the same way, but neither party had said anything. Perhaps if they had been more honest about it, they would still be together.

"How's your latest project coming along?" Rebecca asked, sensing perhaps that a change of conversation was in order.

Katherine relaxed back on to her lounger. "I spoke to the trustee who seems to run the abbey, Margaret. She mulled over what I said and came back to me with a proposal. The trustees want the abbey to be very much part of the village. The next stage of their development plan is converting that old barn that runs down our boundary wall into an event space. Due to the way they had to split the properties, it ended up being on their side."

"Good job too; you don't want the expense of maintaining it. It looks like it's about to fall down."

"They had done some minor work to it at one end as it was the weekend ticket office whilst they built the visitor centre, but yes, otherwise it is pretty dilapidated. Margaret showed me around and went through their plans. They want to start holding weddings next year."

"Good luck to them getting it finished for the spring. Who would book a wedding in there until it could be seen finished?"

"She said they were getting some expert to do some artistic impression, to show off its potential."

"So, how does this affect the village and your dreams of getting pensioners sweaty?"

Katherine twisted her face at the thought.

"She offered out the barn for anything I could throw at it. The nature of the wedding business is of course that you know in advance when you're booked. The rest of the time it would be available to the community, for a small fee of course. She seemed very enthusiastic about it all. They will use it for events as well, but again they will be scheduled well in advance."

"It's going to cost them a fortune to sort it out; I expect

any income from it will help. Don't forget Gloria can always do the catering!"

They caught each other's eye and laughed.

Rebecca continued. "No doubt it will help to have the neighbour on-side when it comes to renovations and late-night parties."

Katherine grinned. "I hadn't thought of that."

"Well, it all sounds perfect. Just one thing concerns me."

Katherine raised her eyebrows and shot her a look.

"You, overdoing it!"

"I think I can cope with a few exercise classes with some pensioners."

The sound of the door knocker reverberated through the kitchen.

"Can you get that?"

"Of course, madam." Rebecca doffed an imaginary hat. "I need to powder my nose anyway."

Katherine went back over everything Margaret had suggested. She was really excited about a new chapter in her life; she was also excited for the abbey. It had so much potential, and she wanted to be part of it. She hadn't told Becks about the most interesting suggestion of Margaret's, as she hadn't yet decided to accept it. Once the GMC debacle was behind her, she could move forward and start making plans.

"You have a visitor, Kat," Rebecca shouted through the kitchen. "I'll make myself scarce."

Katherine got up to see Anna standing by the patio door.

"Anna. To what do I owe the pleasure?"

"Dad says you're not his doctor anymore."

"That's right." Katherine considered giving the reason why but wanted to hear what Anna had to say on the subject before imparting the facts.

Anna joined Katherine on the patio.

"So you ditch us when either of us needs you most. If you were so desperate to be rid of us, I wonder why you even bothered in the first place. We would have been better off without you."

Katherine felt as if she'd been kicked in the gut but tried to keep her cool.

"That's harsh, Anna. You know why I broke it off with you, and you know I'm sorrier than I can say. As for Harry, his care home is well out of our area. It was completely out of my hands. I also understand that his new doctor is particularly experienced with Parkinson's disease, and he has personally reassured me that Harry is in safe hands."

Anna's lips parted and then closed again.

"You know he's stopping there now? He asked to stay. It seems my assistance is no longer required. I can hardly be expected to compete with voice-activated Sky Television, can I?"

Katherine wasn't sure what response she could give that would help the situation. It felt as if Anna was spoiling for a fight, and she was going to do her best not to give her one.

Anna continued. "Well, it seems you've got your way. He's there now, and you were right. I have nothing; no one needs me."

Katherine took a step forward but stopped herself from getting any closer. "Anna, *you* need you, and at this moment you need to pull yourself together and carry on. Deep down you must have seen this coming; it was just a matter of when. It was just a shame that it took Harry falling for it to happen."

Katherine wished away the last sentence as she finished speaking it.

Anna glared at her. "You still hold me responsible for his fall?"

"No. If anyone is responsible it's me. I should have made a better job at getting you to realise he needed a care home rather than making things easier for you and prolonging the inevitable." Katherine's tone intensified. "It seems I was too busy trying to get into your knickers than doing the one job I needed to do, and that was looking out for my patient. At any point, I could have made a call and had him moved, but I didn't, and that's on me. That's why we're not supposed to engage in relationships with patients or their families. It makes us blind!"

Anna's lips parted.

Katherine took a deep breath and then paced the patio. "You might as well know; I wrote to the GMC as soon as Harry was transferred and told them the truth. Don't worry, I said I coerced you into giving a false statement."

Anna's faced dropped in surprise.

"I'm not a liar, Anna — well, not by nature. I'm sorry that I asked you to lie for me; it was unfair. I knew what I was doing; I should have stopped myself."

"What will happen now?" Anna said softly.

"I have a hearing next week. If I'm lucky, I'll get a suspension."

"If not?"

Katherine stopped pacing and faced Anna. "I'll be erased from the register."

They fell into silence.

"Well… good luck. I better go and ring the council and make myself homeless."

Anna turned before Katherine could respond and was gone.

Rebecca reappeared. "Is it safe to come out?"

"Yes." Katherine flopped back onto her lounger. She removed the straw from her glass and took a large swig of Pimm's.

"At least that answers the question of whether she'd speak to you again. What did she want?"

"I'm not sure, to be honest, but I don't like it. I've never seen her like that. I thought she couldn't get more broken."

"Well, you know what we do when we have broken friends."

Katherine looked at Rebecca. "We fix them."

Rebecca nodded.

Katherine wasn't entirely sure how she would even start, but giving Anna a few days to calm down would no doubt be the best course of action.

CHAPTER 26

*K*atherine stopped the timer on her phone. She'd reached the end of the footpath that joined the high street in one hour exactly. That would do for a River Wick walking route and would join three other routes she'd discovered around the village. She strolled along the high street a little slower than she had walked in the last hour, regretting testing all the routes out on the same day. She felt the need for something to repair herself and headed to the tearoom.

"Afternoon, doctor. The usual?"

"Please." Katherine panted, grabbing a chair to rest for a moment.

Gloria disappeared and returned a few minutes later with a smoothie. "I heard you…"

Katherine glared at her. "Yes?"

Gloria thought for a moment. "That you were taking a sabbatical."

Katherine smiled at her and approached the counter. "Yes, I am."

Gloria grinned. "I bet she was worth it, though."

Katherine placed some coins down and picked up her smoothie cup. She walked backwards towards the door. "Totally." She winked at Gloria and sucked her straw to cover her smile. She wondered if she had been wrong about Gloria. It had been at the back of her mind that Gloria had told the GMC, but she knew she'd have to accept that she was unlikely to ever know, and it was best to just let it go.

Gloria chuckled and nodded to the wall beside Katherine. "You might want to take a look at the notice board on your way out, doctor." She disappeared into the back kitchen.

A piece of card was pinned to the centre of the notice board. It read RENTAL WANTED: ONE BEDROOM HOUSE OR HOUSE SHARE IN NUNSWICK/LOCAL AREA, ASAP, CALL ANNA. Katherine recognised the mobile number that accompanied it; it was her Anna, and it seemed she was being evicted. Katherine looked around to check Gloria hadn't reappeared and took the notice off the board.

She looked over at Anna's house as she closed the door of the tearoom. The front door was open, bin bags piled high outside. She'd had about as much space as she could take from Anna; it was time to start fixing things.

Anna was nowhere to be seen as Katherine approached the open front door. She knocked loudly, then stepped inside what was now a largely empty room. An overstuffed bin bag floated down the stairs, Anna attached to it from behind. She stopped as soon as she saw Katherine, then took the last few steps to join her.

Katherine broke the silence. "Hello."

"Hello," Anna replied solemnly.

"You look like you could use some help."

Anna shrugged. "It's nearly done."

"So no reprieve then?"

Anna shook her head. "I have to be out tomorrow." She looked around the room at the furniture that was left. "A clearance van is coming for this lot in the morning."

"I'm sorry, Anna. It must be hard to leave your family home."

Anna nodded.

Katherine could sense her heart was breaking and resisted the urge to pull her into a hug.

"I'm sorry, too, for what I said the other day."

Katherine laughed to try and lighten the mood. "Which bit?"

Anna smirked. "All of it, but particularly about you getting your way with Dad. There was me lecturing you on what was best for him, and you both knew all along. It seems he is thriving at the care home. The irony is he set me free, not the other way around."

"You set each other free. You learned to let each other go."

Anna pulled her lips to one side. "If I hadn't had been so stubborn about Dad, you would never have been put in a position to choose between us. How did it go with the medical council?"

"Twelve months' suspension; they said it would likely have been six if I hadn't lied and coerced you into giving a false statement, but at least I'm still a doctor."

Anna's eyebrows shot up. "Wow, I'm sorry."

"Don't be; now I have time to spend on whatever and whoever I like. It will give me the chance to think about the future and if I want to continue practicing."

"It's been your life. Surely you don't want to give it up?"

Katherine shook her head. "No, helping others is. If you two have taught me anything, it's that I want to be doing more and making a difference in other ways. I want to set up some clubs in the community, get people out walking, organise exercise classes, book clubs. Encourage people to get out of their homes. Sometimes it takes nearly losing something to make you evaluate the worth of it. Being a doctor cost me Helena and you. I don't want to do it anymore if it keeps taking away the things most important to me."

A smile formed on Anna's lips. "I'm proud of you, for what it's worth… for facing the music."

"Thank you. I should have done it all along, and I should have spoken to you. Would you believe me if I told you I've learnt my lesson the hard way?"

Anna nodded. "Yes, I think we both have."

An awkward silence filled the air.

Katherine took a deep breath in; she was encouraged by the apparent truce. "I'm looking for a lodger. Do you know anyone?" Katherine waved the card from the notice board.

Anna shrugged. A corner of her mouth lifted, and she looked at the floor.

Katherine approached Anna and took her hands in hers.

"I have room, Anna. I want you in my life, I want you

in my house, I want you in my bed… because you already have my heart."

The smile growing on Anna's face gave Katherine confidence to continue with her declarations.

"You give me a reason to wake in the morning; I haven't had that in a long time. Waking up next to you… I want to do that every morning."

Anna lunged forward and kissed her lips. "I have nothing to bring to this, nothing except a bag of clothes, a box of books, and" — she looked around — "some family photos that I'm going to need to store."

Katherine broke into a grin. "I have more than enough to share, Anna, and I want to share it all with you."

"How about we start with me renting a room, at a very good rate of course, and maybe we could have a few sleepovers, see how things go?"

"Deal. Virginia will be over the moon. Right, what still needs doing?"

"These black bags need to go outside."

Katherine picked up the bags and took them out.

Anna was examining her dad's chair when Katherine returned. She pushed it to one side, and the back section dropped down. She stepped back. "Shit, I broke Dad's chair."

Katherine looked at it and pulled it away from the wall.

"It looks like it's been broken for some time and was just jammed against the wall to hold it together."

"But I was going to take it to him."

"I don't think this is going anywhere except the tip. I'm sorry."

Katherine wasn't sure if Anna was about to fall to pieces like the chair.

"Well, I suppose it must be older than me. It's always been there for as long as I can remember."

"Let's leave it for the clearance people, shall we?"

Anna nodded.

Katherine looked around. "Anything else?"

Anna pointed to two holdalls. "There's just my stuff and that big box for storing. That smaller box is some things I'm going to take to Dad."

"Is that it?"

"Yep, Dad said he didn't need anything other than his clothes and a few other items. He told me to keep what I wanted, which is in the big box. The rest is going."

"Wow."

"Hmm… one box: the sum total of two people's lives together."

Katherine put her arm around her and rubbed her hand up and down her upper arm. "Come on then, let's go home. Is it too soon for a sleepover tonight?"

Anna laughed. Hearing it made Katherine realise it was one of the things she had missed most about her absence.

CHAPTER 27

*A*s soon as they arrived at Abbey House, Katherine showed Anna to a spare bedroom. Anna set her bags down and collapsed onto the bed.

"I'll let you sort yourself out whilst I make dinner."

Although the room was very comfortable and about six times the size of her room at her dad's, it felt weird being in a different bedroom to Katherine's, having already spent a night in there. Anna was relieved to have a roof over her head. The plan had been to kip on Gloria's floor until she found somewhere more permanent. Now she was going to be living in a sumptuous palace with a beautiful woman.

Katherine's appearance on her doorstep had been a relief to Anna. After her outburst in Katherine's garden and the realisation that Katherine hadn't abandoned her dad, she had been desperate to make amends. Embarrassment had prevented her from approaching Katherine; so much had passed between them, things that shouldn't have been said. It was all now water under the bridge.

Anna made her way downstairs, admiring the staircase again as she went. Katherine was clattering about in the kitchen.

"This isn't going to work," Anna said as she entered.

Katherine's face dropped.

"But… you haven't even stayed a night yet. At least give it a night."

"I mean me staying in a separate room. I'd like to share; I'm assuming the rent will be cheaper too?"

Katherine's relief was audible.

"Why couldn't you have led with that?" She flicked the tea towel she was holding at Anna. "Get some champagne out the fridge."

Anna grinned and extracted a bottle from the fridge, filling the flutes Katherine placed on the island.

Katherine raised hers. "To the future."

"To *our* future," Anna added, chinking her glass. "Do you mind if I have a bath later? I need to wash the day off."

"Of course not. You don't need to ask; this is your home now too. I'll run it for you."

Anna's eyebrows drew together. "You don't need to run me a bath."

"No, but I'd like to."

Anna wasn't going to argue with her, and she was glad she hadn't when she entered the bathroom after dinner. It was lit with endless candles, and the enormous tub, with taps in the middle, was filled with bubbles. She plunged herself into the deep bath and lay back. It was the most luxurious bath she'd ever been in and far surpassed the one in the five-star hotel she'd stayed in once with Jessica.

There was a tap at the door. "Are you decent? Can I come in?" Katherine called.

Anna covered herself with bubbles but then washed them off her chest. She had nothing she didn't want Katherine to see. "Yes, come in?"

Katherine entered with their champagne glasses refilled. "I thought you might like a champagne bath." She stopped, noticing that Anna wasn't as decent as she had expected her to be.

"I won't say no." Anna held out her hand to take it, exposing more of herself.

Katherine was too distracted by Anna's body to notice.

Anna cleared her throat loudly.

"Oh, sorry." She passed a glass to Anna. "I'm going to have a shower."

"Aren't you getting in with me?" Anna teased.

Katherine shot her a look. "Is that a question or an invitation?"

"An invitation of course."

Katherine placed her champagne glass on the side of the bath and dropped her fluffy, white robe to reveal her naked body. She climbed into the other end of the bath.

Anna grinned. "You couldn't have done that quicker if you'd tried."

"Well, I didn't want you to change your mind."

"Oh, there's no fear of that," Anna replied, her grin lifting into a smile. She was sure Katherine was blushing. It took all her willpower not to throw herself across the bath onto Katherine and her beautiful body. Even naked she had an air of confidence. Anna couldn't believe she was all hers for the taking.

They shifted their legs to make themselves comfortable, giving each other little smirks as they touched.

"You know earlier, how I mentioned my future and what I'm going to do?" Katherine asked. "Well, before I finalise anything, I want to run it past you first."

"Good." Anna smirked at her, and Katherine narrowed her eyes in return.

"Well, in addition to starting some community classes, which I'm going to hold in the new barn — "

"At the abbey?" Anna interrupted.

"Yes," Katherine replied taking a sip of Champagne.

Anna's eyes lit up. "Margaret showed me the plans; it looks like it will be an amazing space for the abbey and the community."

"I agree. Margaret mentioned something else to me when I discussed my ideas with her. One of the trustees is stepping down, and she'd like me to take over."

Anna sat forward. "Wow."

"Hmm."

"Would this be instead of being a doctor?"

Katherine twisted her lips and nodded. "Yes, I think it would, but I have a year to decide for certain. The way they set the trust up allows them to pay their trustees, so I would get a salary from it."

"Okay, this is sounding too good to be true. What's the catch?"

"Investment."

"Ahh. A large investment?" Anna questioned.

"Sizeable but affordable. As you know, my mother left me with a sizable sum, but what I haven't told you is Becks made a case against the driver that killed Helena. This added substantially to the sum. I haven't touched any of it. I wanted to do something worthwhile with it, use it to bring enjoyment and pleasure to others."

Anna nodded her agreement. "What would you be doing in return for the salary?"

"Overseeing the development and management of the new barn."

Anna frowned. "Are you qualified for that?"

"I've run urgent treatment centres. I think a medieval barn could be considered trivial compared to that."

Anna nodded. "Agreed. What does Rebecca say to all this? I assume you'll need her permission."

"I haven't mentioned it yet. I thought we could decide together and then let her know."

"If this is what you want, then we'll make it work."

Katherine placed her glass on the side of the bath and shifted herself onto her knees between Anna's legs. The water lapped at her breasts, and her nipples cut through the bubbles as she closed in on Anna. She took the glass from Anna's hand and leaned back to place it with hers. Anna's heart pounded at the view this presented.

As Katherine approached her again, Anna reached out to caress both her breasts. Katherine writhed at her touch and breathed in deeply. She rested her arms on the sides of the bath and lowered herself to meet Anna's face, her blue eyes boring deep into hers.

"I love you, Anna Walker."

Anna pushed her lips together to moisten them.

"I love you too…" Anna's eyes flashed sideways and then back to Katherine. "Kat?"

Katherine's smile told Anna she had chosen wisely, and the pace of her breath quickened. Anna could feel the warmth of it against her cool, wet skin. Anna inhaled slowly to control her own spiralling breath.

"Only those very close to me get to call me that."

Anna looked at the space between their bodies. "Admittedly, we could be closer."

Katherine lowered her body onto Anna's, letting her legs slide back. Her breasts crushed themselves against Anna's. Their eyes locked, noses touched, and their lips, millimetres apart, pressed together firmly.

CHAPTER 28

*A*nna woke to the touch of Katherine's lips on hers. She recalled the previous night and smiled, pulling Katherine closer. "Morning."

There was a muffled mewing sound between them.

"Sorry, Virginia." Katherine pulled back.

Anna watched as Virginia curled back up and shut her eyes.

"Are we supposed to work around her?"

"It's her bed as much as ours, I'm afraid. She could actually lay full claim to it as she spends more time in it than I do."

"Well, we're going to have to change that, aren't we?" Anna swept a strand of Katherine's hair behind her ear and leaned forward, planting a kiss on her lips. "You're more beautiful than ever in the morning."

Katherine blushed. "So are you. I was going to suggest we have a re-run of last night but…" They both looked down at Virginia who was watching them with one eye open.

"Perhaps not, eh?" Anna checked her phone beside the bed. "Shit, I forgot to set an alarm; the clearance guys will be waiting. I better get over there."

Anna jumped out of bed and dressed under the examining eye of Katherine.

"It's rude to stare." Anna grinned, pleased to have the attention.

"Only if the stare is unwanted."

Anna walked around to Katherine's side of the bed and sat down. She leaned into her and kissed her, sliding her hand under the duvet.

Katherine moaned at her touch. "Do you have to go right now?"

"Honestly, there is no place I'd rather be than under that duvet, but they are going to be waiting for me." Anna removed her hand and walked to the door. "Do you want to come along in a bit? Make sure I actually leave the place?"

"Sure, give me an hour."

"You finish up." She winked at Katherine and left.

As Anna stepped out of the house, she nearly trod on a bunch of flowers. She picked them up and examined them; a card was inside.

She returned to the bedroom and presented them to Katherine who was still in bed and stroking Virginia.

"Oh, you shouldn't have!" Katherine said. Then she studied the envelope and added, "Hang on — you didn't."

"No, not me, sorry. Must be one of your other admirers."

"Most likely, I have many." Katherine took the card from the flowers and opened it. "Oh."

"Oh?" Anna questioned.

Katherine handed the card to Anna.

"Dear Katherine, I very much hope we'll be working much closer together in the future. Perhaps we can do dinner sometime. M x." Anna looked at Katherine and raised her eyebrows. "Something I should know?"

"Don't ask me. I must pop in and see her anyway to accept the job. I'll check there hasn't been any misunderstanding."

"You do that; I'm not sharing you with anyone. I didn't even know she was a lesbian." Anna tilted her head. "Come to think of it, though, I probably did."

"It doesn't necessarily mean what you think it means," Katherine said.

"Well, good luck finding out. I'll see you later."

The clearance guys were climbing out of their van as she arrived, and with pleasantries and instructions given to clear everything, they set about their work.

Anna leaned against the wall and watched them as one by one they removed her memories from the house. A welcome distraction appeared in the doorway in the shape of Katherine.

"How's it going?"

"Nearly done."

"Sorry I took so long. I cleared out the bedside table, some drawers, and hanging space in the dressing room for you."

"Thank you." She kissed Katherine.

A loud cough took their attention to the guy in charge, who'd entered the room.

"We're all done; everything was as agreed, so I'll make

the transfer as soon as I get back to the office. If you could sign this, please." He handed over a clipboard; Anna gave it a cursory look and signed it.

"Thanks."

He nodded and left.

"I'll just do a last check before we go."

Katherine nodded. "I'll be here."

Anna went upstairs and wandered around the empty rooms; the small sound she made echoed against the walls. In her old bedroom, she remembered the time she'd made a pass at another girl she liked only to be rejected and laughed at. She'd come home and cried her eyes out, curled up in the corner.

She ran her fingers over the wall next to where her bed had been. She felt the shape of a heart that she had etched into the wall when she got her first girlfriend. She had been desperate to mark the occasion somehow, and as her mum and dad didn't know at the time that she was into girls, a small marking on the wall felt fitting. Neither her mum nor dad knew she had done it, or if they did, they had never said anything.

She made her way across the landing to her parents' bedroom. She could visualise her mum in the bed, as she did every time she had entered it since, writhing in pain. Anna had been home that weekend and called the ambulance, knowing it wasn't just indigestion. She'd never returned home, as she had been taken to the care home a week after her cancer diagnosis.

Trying to recall happier times, Anna took her mind back to jumping on their bed in the mornings and them both pretending to be asleep, only to jump at her and tickle her until she screamed.

Anna wiped her eyes and headed downstairs.

"Are you ready?" Katherine asked.

Anna shook her head. "I need to do one more thing." She pressed her ear to the wall.

Katherine smiled at her. "What can you hear?"

"I can hear my mum shouting at my dad to turn the television off and come and sit at the table for his dinner." Tears rolled from her eyes.

Katherine took her hand and squeezed it. "What else?"

"My dad telling me that if I run down the stairs and break my legs, I'm not to come running to him." She laughed through the tears.

Katherine pulled her away from the wall. "Can you still hear it?"

Anna nodded and wiped her eyes with her sleeve.

"I'm not saying voices aren't absorbed into the walls, even science wouldn't refute that, but they're absorbed into people, too, and we can carry them everywhere we go. The voices have long gone from these walls, but they're never gone from here." Katherine lifted Anna's hand and placed it on her chest. "Ready?"

Anna smiled. "Yes, I think I am." She took one last look around the room as Katherine stepped outside. "Bye, Mum." She wiped her eyes, took a deep breath, and followed Katherine outside.

"Okay?"

Anna shoved the key through the letterbox. "Yes, I am."

Katherine held her hand out to Anna. "As one door closes, another opens."

Anna smiled and took her hand. "What do we do now?"

Katherine pulled her closer. "Anything you like."

"I want to visit Dad. Will you come?"

"Of course, though I'll need your help getting something in the car first."

They held hands as they walked along the high street back to Abbey House. It felt good to have the doctor on her arm, and any shocked faces were met with big smiles from both her and Katherine. Nunswick was going to have to get used to two ladies walking around holding hands in public and occasionally kissing outside the tearoom.

"So, how did it go with Margaret? Are you now my boss?" Anna asked.

"I am indeed, and before you ask, the card wasn't what you thought. She was very embarrassed that I might have taken it that way, which, come to think of it, I probably wouldn't have if you hadn't suggested it."

"Did you disclose our relationship before or after you brought it up?"

"I mentioned it when I accepted the job; she said it wouldn't be a problem."

"So she knew we were together before you confronted her about the card."

Katherine laughed. "Yes, what of it?"

"Only that she would hardly admit it meant something else when you'd just told her you were seeing me."

Katherine's tone changed. "She appeared genuinely mortified, so that's enough for me. Let's drop it."

Anna didn't feel she could push the point any further. She hoped rather than believed that Margaret had at least got the message and that would be an end to it.

"That reminds me: she asked me to give you something." Katherine rummaged in her bag and extracted a rectangular packet. "Congratulations."

Anna extracted a guidebook from the packet and flicked through the pages. "It's better than I imagined." A wide smile spread across her face, and she stuffed her nose into the book, inhaling deeply.

Katherine laughed at her. "I'm glad I'm not the only one that sniffs books." She opened the boot of her car remotely as they approached the driveway and pulled a catch inside, which dropped the back seats.

"I'm intrigued," Anna said as Katherine extracted the boot cover.

The corners of Katherine's mouth curled. "Come on, I'll show you."

Anna followed Katherine into the house.

"Are you serious?" Anna stared at the large leather chair in Katherine's sitting room. "That won't fit in your car."

"We can at least try. I'd been thinking about buying two new chairs; you could help me choose."

"I won't say no, although I did enjoy cuddling up on your long sofas." Anna nudged herself into Katherine.

"Perhaps we should just move the television instead then?"

"Let's see if we can get this in the car first, shall we? Or even out the front door."

With a lot of heavy breathing and pulled muscles, they

squeezed the chair into the boot of the car. They held their breath as the boot came down and, with a slight movement on the chair's part, shut.

"Here, you can drive." Katherine threw a bunch of keys at Anna. "I'm quite done being the chauffeur."

"But I'm not insured."

"You are as of this morning. I took a photo of your driver's licence… when we were… before. I was going to do it then."

Anna narrowed her eyes. "You're sneaky. I'm going to have to watch you."

"I can't promise I won't surprise you or treat you to things; it's my nature, and you're going to have to put up with it. You can keep that key. It's yours now, and there's a set of keys for the house too."

Anna smirked. "You *are* serious about me, Dr Atkinson."

"I couldn't be more serious, Miss Walker."

When they arrived at Baycroft, Lucy informed them that Harry was in the games room with his friends. They took the opportunity, assisted by several staff members, to move the chair into his room. Anna clung to the box of possessions from the house.

Once in position, Lucy stood back and admired it. "He's going to like that; he's not stopped groaning about his current one."

Anna placed the box on the bed and opened it. She took out an urn and positioned it in the centre of the windowsill, beside the chair. She placed two photo frames on either side of it — one of the three of them together when Anna was a small child and the second with Anna in her late teens.

Katherine hugged her. "That's really sweet. Let's go and find him."

They made their way through the atrium to the games room where Lucy said they would likely find Harry.

Katherine gazed at the roof of the atrium "This place is amazing."

"You can see why he didn't want to leave," Anna replied.

"I'm not sure I want to either."

"Give it a couple of years and they'll probably take you."

Katherine nudged at Anna with her elbow. "Oi!"

Anna grinned as she peered through the glass window. Harry spotted her and beckoned her in; she took Katherine's hand as she entered. All the eyes in the room turned to look at them.

"Everyone, this is my daughter and her — " He lowered his eyes to their conjoined hands and smiled. "And her girlfriend, Katherine."

Anna squeezed Katherine's hand and felt her squeeze back. She didn't realise she would be so nervous having her dad introduce them to his friends. Everyone raised a hand or smiled at them.

"I'll see you chaps later; I've got two ladies to entertain."

Anna wheeled him out of the games room and back to his. They stopped at the door.

"Katherine's got a surprise for you, Dad."

"We've got a surprise for you," Katherine corrected her.

Katherine opened the door, and Anna pushed Harry through.

"I recognise that chair. I hope you threw that other one away."

"I think they'll use it in another room, Dad."

Harry pushed himself to his feet and shuffled to it before collapsing onto it in contentment.

"Ahh, that's much better." He winked at Katherine, and she winked back. "So you two took your time sorting things out." He looked at Katherine. "Have you moved her in with you?"

Katherine put her arm around Anna and pulled her in. "I have indeed."

"Better late than never, I say. You'll look after her for me, won't you, doc?"

"I will, Harry."

"Dad, you have to stop calling her doc; she might not be a doctor for much longer anyway."

"You were a good doc to me, but I'd rather have you as a daughter-in-law any day of the week."

"Dad." Anna perched on the table and tapped him on the arm.

Katherine sniggered. "Subtle, Harry. Very subtle."

"Well, whenever you get around to it. What matters is that now I get to see you both, and more importantly" — he slowly lifted his arm and pointed at Anna's face — "I get to see that smile."

Anna took his shaking hand and placed it on the arm of the chair, keeping her hand on top of it.

"Look, Dad." Anna pointed at the urn. "I've brought Mum to stay with you."

"I noticed. Thanks, love. So the house has gone now then?"

Anna nodded, failing to hold back tears.

"There, there, love; life moves on and we must with it. It won't be long before you two are in here, tearing the place up with your gal pals. Make the most of life and each other; that's what your mum would have said."

Anna nodded and wiped her eyes.

"No more tears, eh?"

Anna smiled at him. "No more tears."

As they left the care home an hour later, Anna hooked herself onto Katherine's arm and leaned into her as they walked to the car. She felt truly free of the feeling of foreboding that had been her constant companion for many months. The ache in the pit of her stomach had been replaced by butterflies.

Katherine turned to her as they reached the car. "Let's go and make some new memories."

Anna nodded. "Bagsy! I drive," she shouted as she ran around to the driver's side.

"I'm never driving this car again, am I?"

Anna shook her head and smiled.

THE END

If you enjoyed this book, please consider leaving me a review on Amazon, BookBub or Goodreads. Just a rating or a line is fine. Reviews are life-blood to authors, boosting visibility and connecting new readers with our books.

Amazon review link…

Keep turning to find out more about Anna and Katherine's Christmas antics in Trust in Truth!

JOIN MY READERS CLUB

If you'd like to hear about my new releases, sign up to my newsletter and receive a FREE sapphic romance,
The Third Act…

At the suggestion of her daughter, Amy, widowed Fiona attends an art course at the local college where she meets the confident, inspirational teacher, Raye.
Raye awakens feelings long suppressed, but as Fiona rediscovers her sexuality, fear grows over how Amy will react.
Can Fiona find the courage to follow her heart, or will she be destined to spend her third act alone?

5* - Absolutely loved this book! Great story line, well developed characters and beautifully crafted. It is really refreshing to see the older lesbian represented for a change!

www.emilybanting.co.uk/freebook

NUNSWICK ABBEY SERIES
BOOK TWO

TRUST IN TRUTH - A CHRISTMAS NOVELLA

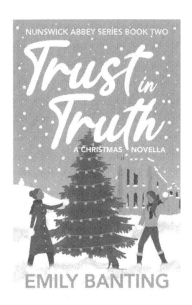

Spend the season in Nunswick with TRUST IN TRUTH, the enthralling follow-up to LOST IN LOVE.

After the events of the summer, Katherine and Anna are looking forward to spending a quiet, cosy Christmas together before hosting a New Year's Eve party at Nunswick Abbey.

When a romantic weekend away for Anna's birthday doesn't go to plan, it proves to be the beginning of their

Christmas woes, and as workplace pleasantries grow too friendly, a cloud of jealousy and suspicion forms.

As Anna plans the most important party of her career, can she convince Katherine their co-worker has more than pub lunches on the brain? Can Katherine keep her composure as the tension rises at Abbey House?

As TRUST IN TRUTH counts down to the New Year, will Anna and Katherine's relationship survive the calamitous Christmas season?

Available on Amazon...

EMILY BANTING

Sydney MacKenzie, personal assistant to the rich and famous, is looking forward to a well-earned break to go travelling in her beloved VW camper van, Gertie — that is, until Gertie cries off sick. When her boss calls in a favour, one that will pay Sydney handsomely and put Gertie back on the road, she can't refuse.

Internationally renowned actress Beatrice Russell — adored by her fans and despised by those that know her — is splashed across the tabloids, all thanks to her broken leg.

She limps back to her palatial English country estate to convalesce for the summer, where she finds herself in need of yet another new assistant.

Enter Sydney, who doesn't take kindly to the star's demands, attitude, or clicking fingers — much less her body's own attraction to the gorgeous diva. If not for that, and Gertie's worn-out engine, she would leave tomorrow. Or so she tells herself.

As the summer heats up, the ice queen begins to thaw, and Sydney glimpses the tormented woman beneath the celebrity bravado, drawing her ever closer to the enigmatic actress — sometimes too close.

Can Sydney reach the real Beatrice and help heal her wounds before the summer ends and she returns to filming in the States, or is the celebrity broken beyond repair?

Available on Amazon.

GOODREADS REVIEWS

"One of the best books I've ever read, period!"

★★★★★

"I have read over 200 books this year. This is the best

written book of the year for me."

"Oh. My. God. I couldn't put this book down."

"One of the best books I've read in a long time."

"This book spoke to me and I wish there were some way to make it required reading. The emotional and social insights are wonderful even when difficult."

Syd and Beatrice are supported by a cast of some of the most beautifully developed side characters I've seen.

Printed in Great Britain
by Amazon